OVER MY DEAD HUSBAND'S BODY

ETTA FAIRE

CHAPTER 1

DEAD SERIOUS

*W*hen I left this town, I told everyone I'd rather burn alive in a septic tank fire than return. My good friend Shelby Winehouse walked me out to my car that day, carrying the last box of crap that I didn't really need but wasn't about to leave for my ex.

She turned and hugged me. "Come on, Carly Mae. You're joking. You'll at least come back to visit."

I couldn't get the words out fast enough. "I am dead serious. I would rather suffocate in a blaze of toxic shit fumes than come back here. No offense. We'll still keep in touch. But everyone knows my business. Everyone knows what happened with Jackson. I'm not coming back."

That was four years ago. And we hadn't kept in touch.

I flipped off the sign sign I was passing.

Potter Grove, Wisconsin, population 1,500.

No point in searching out flammable port-a-potties now.

My car bumped and swerved, hitting every pothole and crevice along the way. I could hear my ex-husband laughing in his grave somewhere, wherever he was buried. I absolutely refused to look that one up. He was the reason I was back here. The bastard.

When I got the call about three weeks ago, I was down in my mother's basement in Indianapolis. My mother was busy telling me, once again, how I needed to Xerox more resumes to mail out to temp agencies, and I had just finished thanking her for her unsolicited career advice from 1986, when my phone rang. I hadn't known the number and suspected spam, but I answered anyway, just to stop my mother from going on and on about how I needed to buy a navy skirt for job interviews.

"It just presents better than black."

"I have to take this," I said, like it was someone important. After confirming my identity, the man on the other end matter-of-factly told me he was the lawyer representing Jackson Bowman's estate.

"His estate?"

"Yes, ma'am. Your late ex-husband..."

I hadn't even known he'd died, but apparently, it had been months. I pulled the phone away and stared at it, not really hearing what the man was saying anymore. I'd spent a good part of the last four years of my life dreaming about that day. I'd even choreographed a short jig for it, but somehow, I didn't feel like dancing anymore.

I pulled into the coffee shop before I made my way up the long, steep dirt drive to Gate House. Might as well rip this band-aid off as soon as possible. I parked next to the pink Cadillac I knew was Shelby's. She still drove the same beat-up car she pretended she got from selling makeup. We all knew she won it at an auction in Landover and had it painted that color. Makeup companies didn't give out 60s Cadillacs with dents.

The coffee shop was the same as I'd remembered: Jukebox playing Elvis Presley. The smell of grease and cheese wafting up from the kitchen, Spoony River's specialties.

Mrs. Carmichael stood at the back of the counter, her short puffy blonde hair sticking out in all the wrong directions from her uniform's little pink hat. She was one of the few people I truly missed. My old best friend's mom. She didn't look up when I entered. "Try to find a spot," she laughed, gesturing around at the empty tables and chairs set up to look like a 50s diner.

Old George, the town's barber, sat at the end of the counter, the only other customer in the place besides me. He glanced up from his newspaper and his sunken, ashen face dropped with surprise. "Look what survived the septic tank fire," he said, making me realize I really did tell everyone that. "Carly Mae, I heard you were coming back. But I did not believe it."

"It's just Carly now," I replied, my voice softer than I'd meant.

Mrs. Carmichael squealed herself into a smoker's cough when she saw me. She hacked her way across the restaurant, waving her thick arms around like she couldn't wait to give me one of her famous bear hugs, same as she gives everybody but you always feel special when you're on the receiving end. "I knew you'd come back." She looked me over. "Tina always told me, 'Mom, people don't leave Potter Grove. It snatches you like quicksand.'" She scrunched her eyes when she mentioned Tina, and I searched her face to see if she was mad I hadn't called. I should've called.

Every part of me knew the etiquette now was to ask how Tina was doing. Instead, I dug one of my Nikes into the checkerboard plastic tiled floor. "It also helps to come back if your dead ex-husband gives you a free house."

"And that's why, Carly Mae, you are the luckiest ex-wife I know." It was Shelby peeking her head through the little serving hatch that led to the kitchen. "A dead ex-husband and a free house? That's better than the Lotto." Shelby was only saying that because she'd rather have dead exes than dead-beat ones. She had four kids and two divorces. But it did feel a lot like a lottery win for me too.

She hurried out from the kitchen. Her hair was pink now, same shade as her car, and she was pregnant again.

Shelby turned me around, making me self-conscious all of the sudden. It had been a long car ride from Indianapolis and I probably should've checked my hair and makeup before I stopped in, especially since this woman was always on the prowl for a new customer.

She sucked in a thin lip. "I should give you a makeover," she began. She pulled on one of my brownish blonde curls then watched it spring back into place. "There's a hair care product line now." She turned her head to the side like I was a blank canvas.

"She just got here, Shelby," Mrs. Carmichael interrupted. "For goodness sakes, let the poor girl rest her pocket book a second."

Old George checked his watch then put his hat on. "Shoot. I gotta go. Brock's comin' in for a trim. Boy likes his hair too long if you ask me," he said while grabbing his jacket from off the back of the chair. His barber shop was right next door, and it was a beautiful day in July, but old George walked around like a blizzard might break out at any moment.

"Brock's still single," Shelby sing-songed as old George left.

"Mrs. Carmichael calls him the Hunk. You know, instead of the Hulk. Isn't that right, Mrs. Carmichael?"

Mrs. Carmichael looked down at her pink dress, smoothing out the wrinkles along its pleats. Shelby seemed to catch her mistake and quickly went on. "We have a lot of good prospects here. Justin Fortworth's also single and... okay, maybe just the two."

Brock Calhoun was probably the best looking guy in Potter Grove, or at least he used to be back when I worked with him at the Thriftway in college. But he was also Tina's ex. And Mrs. Carmichael was Tina's mom.

Shelby carefully wiggled onto the stool next to me. "But, there used to be three eligible bachelors. One hunk is no longer on the market." She patted her baby bump, and held out her hand to show me her engagement ring, a tiny blue stone that looked like glass. "Bobby Franklin, if you can believe it." I could. Bobby Franklin was the town ne'er-do-well, always leaving town for some sort of life-changing opportunity he'd heard about. Still, I never thought he was the type to give out engagement rings. I hugged her. "Congratu-lations."

"Another boy," she said.

Mrs. Carmichael untied the straps of her apron, sat down, then retied them again. The apron still looked like it cut off her circulation. "You might not know this, Carly Mae, but we've had some trouble here in Potter Grove. And I don't just mean the fact you've got a lot of people none too happy Jackson left you his house."

I knew exactly who she was talking about. Destiny was one of those people who was none too happy, which made me all too happy. She was Jackson's wife at the time of his death, and the reason we got divorced in the first place, mostly because she was the stripper I caught him with. And Jackson's family was probably none too happy either. The Victorian had been in their family for generations.

I had no idea why my ex left me his creepy old house. Didn't care much, though, either. A free house was a free house.

"Murder," Mrs. Carmichael said, and I almost fell off my stool, knocked out of my smug daydream.

"What?" Potter Grove didn't have a *crime rate*. "Are you serious?"

"Dead serious," Shelby replied. "Don't trust anyone."

"Stop scaring her." Mrs. Carmichael said. "But, you need to watch yourself, that's all. Lock the doors. Be careful at night. All women around here need to. Two women from Landover went missing a little more than a year ago," Mrs. Carmichael said, shaking her head. "They turned up dead here in Potter Grove."

Shelby took up where Mrs. Carmichael left off. "Two more went missing earlier this year. No trace of them, yet. Police say it's a hate crime against women. So, be careful. Maybe get some mace. And a knife, or a gun. Lots of concealed weapons."

I must've looked as pale as I felt because Mrs. Carmichael shushed Shelby. "I said stop scaring her. You're gonna give the poor girl a heart attack, like Jackson."

I hadn't known how Jackson died until that very moment. I never bothered to look it up. I should've guessed that was how the old man went out, though. Jackson had been a heavy drinker who was more than twenty years my senior.

But now, after hearing about the attacks on women, I wasn't sure I wanted a free house in Landover County. I checked my watch. It was after 2:00, the time I was supposed to meet Jackson's lawyer. I hugged Mrs. Carmichael and

Shelby good-bye then rushed out the door. Once again, I hadn't asked about Tina. I never managed to get that done.

My shoes sounded extra heavy smacking along the concrete on my way out to my car. The parking lot seemed too empty and quiet. I turned my head in every direction possible, checking the surrounding woods, gasping to myself every time a bird rustled through the branches overhead.

I was about to move into a creepy, weird Victorian that sat at the very top of a deserted hill, with a murderer on the loose. And it was all my ex-husband's fault. He was getting the last laugh in death too.

CHAPTER 2

YOU GET WHAT YOU PAY FOR

The drive up to Gate House wasn't easy, but I knew this ahead of time and popped a motion pill a while back. The path, full of twists and turns along a hill-like mountain of dirt, had never been given much of a facelift over the years. There weren't any signs posted to indicate this was Gate Hill, no lights along the way to guide anyone coming or going at night. No wonder the lawyer insisted on meeting in the afternoon. He probably knew he'd end up in a ditch at any other time. And now, all of this creepiness was mine. With a murderer on the loose.

The trees that surrounded the road seemed to get closer at every turn, like throat muscles closing in to swallow prey. The afternoon sun was barely visible through the overhanging branches. I checked the speedometer and pushed the gas pedal up to to 20 miles per hour, causing my car to bounce over every rock and hole like it was having one major accident after another. I took a deep breath. I could do this, again and again. Every day for the rest of my life.

The entire seven years I was married to Jackson, I begged

him to get an apartment in the city. We both worked at the university in Landover, the "big city" by Potter Grove, and it was bad enough coming home from a long day's work without having to inch my way up Spooky Mountain just to relax.

"What?" he would yell like getting an apartment was the dumbest thing I could've said. "We have the chance to live in a beautiful, historical Victorian designed by my great grandfather, and you want to get an apartment?"

He used the word "beautiful" loosely a lot when describing this place. It was a crazy house designed by a crazy person, who everyone politely labeled "eccentric" because, apparently, you shouldn't call rich people crazy. Gate House had been in the Bowman family for forever, named Gate House because, aside from the massive hill you had to drive up, there were also two security gates to pass through before you even spotted a turret. The old man was paranoid about something. Eccentric all right. Eccentric out of his flipping mind.

I moved forward, past the first gate, a rusty, pocked iron one straight out of a horror movie.

As soon as I could afford it, I was going to change some things around my "new" house. I pictured my ex rolling over in his grave as he watched me messing with his stuff.

Good. I didn't know why he left me everything anyway. We hadn't even spoken since he called to tell me he was marrying Destiny, which was an odd conversation, to say the least.

"Carly doll, I have wonderful news. I'm getting married again, to Destiny the stripper." I could hear Destiny cackling in the background. They were both drunk.

I hung up without even offering a "Congratulations."

Apparently, eccentricity runs in some families, and I was just happy we hadn't had any children.

Gate House came into view, exactly as I remembered it. It was not the traditional Victorian, probably because it was designed by a madman who never took an architectural course in his life. There was one main turret that actually looked like two turrets plopped one on top of the other, and three little ones just for show that didn't hold much. Each had its own entrance, detached from the main house. The guy had a thing for turrets.

Ronald, Jackson's lawyer, was a wax-mustached twig with slightly more twitches than he had pens in his shirt pocket, but then, I really didn't count either. Waiting for me outside, he paced the dark green veranda back and forth, making a circular motion in the air with one of his fingers when he saw me pull up, probably in an effort to get me to hurry up.

"You're half an hour late," he snapped, like he expected me to pay him, or apologize. Neither was going to happen. I agreed to two-o'clock-ish, and only because he'd insisted. I'd just driven seven hours straight from Indianapolis to Potter Grove. I had a car full of my entire belongings and I think I may have smelled a little like Dr. Pepper from a soda explosion somewhere around Chicago. He never even asked how my trip went. Did I hit much traffic? Did I make good time? As soon as my foot hit the first step of the porch, he thrust a stack of papers at me and a pen.

"I was on my way out, actually. I thought you'd forgotten. Like I said before I have to fly out of here at 3:30 and we have a lot to discuss," he said. "First and foremost..."

I heard a familiar sound and Ronald lost my attention again.

Rex, our Labrador and the only thing I missed about my

marriage to Jackson, sprinted across the front lawn over to me. I swear the dog was smiling.

I hugged him hard, running my hands through his short golden fur. "I missed you too," I said, over and over again.

Ronald continued talking like I was listening. "There's a stipend of two thousand dollars a month while you take care of Rex."

"A stipend," I said, actually listening now. "Did you say two thousand?" That was more than I'd ever made freelance writing horrible articles from my mother's basement. Hot damn! Maybe I'd be able to tackle my novel after all.

Ronald continued in his monotone voice. "We've gone over this before, Ms. Taylor, please try to keep up. That's to cover utilities and expenses for Rex."

I remembered how much expenses were for a house of this size, and a couple thousand dollars was pretty bare-boned. I would have to get a side job while I wrote my book after all.

"Rex's schedule is outlined on page two. Please initial at the bottom that you agree to all terms..."

I flipped over to page two and scribbled my initials without bothering to look over anything. Ronald had to fly out of here at 3:30 and I had to keep up, after all.

Rex eagerly pushed his head into my hand as I made a mostly for-show attempt at reading whatever it was Ronald was pointing out to me. The dog's large dark eyes looked up at me in the same playful way as the day I met him, even though he had to be old, very old. His little scarred nose shot through my hand again and again. I definitely got the feeling he was trying to tell me something.

I always told Jackson that Rex was the smartest dog in the world. He dropped something hard and smooth into my hand then stood back and panted, waiting for me to pay attention to him. I missed him, too, from his lopsided ears to the little V-shaped scar on the tip of his nose. "In a minute, big guy. I promise we'll catch up or play fetch or whatever you want." I mindlessly shoved the thing he gave me into my pocket and tried to keep up with the fast-talking lawyer.

"Now, onto the house agreement."

"House agreement?" I said. "This is my house, right? As in, I agree to do whatever the hell I want with it like sell it or burn it, mostly sell it."

Ronald tapped his antique Rolex.

I stopped talking and paid attention.

"To boil it down," he said, turning toward the door that led to the kitchen, making his now-famous circular finger motion so I'd quickly follow him inside. "Everything. Everything's protected under this agreement. Not a single antique or piece of hand-crafted wallpaper can be sold... or burned, or else the entire agreement is null and void. You are to receive this house under the conditions that you take care of Rex without changing a thing until the dog's demise. Rex is very sensitive to change."

He pointed around the kitchen first, which was exactly like the day I left it, everything in gorgeous dark thick mahogany with ornamental designs carved into the wood-work. He opened one of the cabinets above the counter. I tried to remember what was in there -- water glasses and coffee mugs. I peeked in. I was right.

"You will see on pages four through eighteen that a detailed count has been made of all the china, glasses, goblets, silverware, stoneware..."

I stared at the pages that listed everything in the kitchen along with the place at the bottom of each page I was supposed to initial to say that everything was correct to the best of my knowledge and that I wouldn't change a thing. I should've known there'd be a stack of paperwork the size of an old phonebook to sign to get this place. The prenup I'd signed had been equally as thick. I was a fool to sign that eleven years ago, and here I was about to be the fool again.

Ronald saw me checking ahead through the agreement. "He's an old dog," he said, his voice finally rising out of its monotone, like he was trying to project optimism. "He won't last long, I'm sure. And then, at that time, the house is yours to burn."

I looked down at my Lab. I'd rather have him alive. The only reason I hadn't fought for Rex during the divorce was because I knew I'd never get him. Jackson had owned Rex when I met him almost 12 years ago, and he hadn't been a puppy.

Rex followed at my heels as I walked around the kitchen, and a thought occurred to me: How would anyone know if I accidentally threw out a fork or sold an antique tea set to help pay for electricity? This dog wasn't talking.

Ronald seemed to read my mind. "Mrs. Harpton will be here on Thursdays and Mondays to clean and inspect the place to make sure the contract is still in good standing. Come along," he said. "We have more to discuss and I have to fly out of here soon."

We went from room to room as the lawyer droned on, each sentence more of a life sentence than the last.

"And you will take no more than three weeks of vacation a year, completely at your discretion, but allowing Mrs. Harpton ample time to make arrangements. You are expected to be here all other nights."

"All other nights?" I repeated. "You can't mean that. What if I get a boyfriend?"

The lawyer's alarm chimed on his phone. He chuckled, pulling it out of his pants pocket. "About the only thing a cell-phone's good for around here since there's no coverage, I'm afraid. I've got to go. Remember, the phone people will be here tomorrow to install your landline around 11:00, cable and Internet too. I'll transfer the utilities bill next week."

He patted Rex's head then, after looking and seeing me scanning through the agreement, made a mock-signing motion to show me what I should be doing. I quickly initialed and signed the last few pages where spots were highlighted and handed the thick stack of papers back to him. The terms were weird, and restrictive, but I could always decline the inheritance later if I decided I couldn't stand it. Give the place to one of the people who were none too happy with me getting it.

But right now, I needed a house, a place away from my mother and her constant reminders that I was a 31-year-old failure without a husband, kids, or a career she could brag about at bingo. I also missed Rex, and in a way, this town. As creepy as it all was, it was also familiar and comforting.

As soon as the lawyer left, I plopped down on the rich Victorian settee in the living room and ran a hand over its crimson fabric, which was in remarkably good shape for its age, no tears or stains, no discoloration. It was funny. I could almost hear my ex-husband's pretentious, snotty voice, calling me from the kitchen. "Carly doll, you burned the pizza again. Why do you buy those frozen, awful things, anyway?"

My stomach growled. And I almost cried. *Pizza*. I hadn't thought about groceries. I was in such a hurry to get here on time for a weird lawyer who'd just made me sign my life away that I'd forgotten to buy food. I'm sure Destiny hadn't left me anything to eat in this place that wasn't thoroughly seasoned with arsenic. I'd have to drive back down the hill or starve. I couldn't do it, not after driving seven hours straight. I leaned my head against the pillow, a frustrated tear falling down my cheek.

"Awww, how sweet," said a snotty familiar voice. "I miss me too."

CHAPTER 3

DEAD, BUT NOT FORGIVEN

I screamed and rolled off the settee, hitting the dogwood-patterned rug underneath, fully awake now despite the motion pill I took and my exhaustion. "Jackson?" I said, looking around the room. My throat went dry and I could hardly get my voice to work right.

What looked like the dark figure of my ex-husband appeared in the shadows near the entrance to the kitchen. I closed my eyes for a full three seconds then opened them again. He was still there. A very faded version. His color was weak and strange as he stood in the entryway. Or, was he standing?

"Did you fake your death?" I whispered.

I moved closer to him, blinking my eyes, telling myself my mind was just overly tired.

The thing by the kitchen was Jackson, all right. I was able to make out the beard he always claimed wasn't pretentious even though he had a special comb for it and the tweed jacket with the elbow patches he liked to wear because it made him look like "a walking cliche of an English professor." No one ever understood his jokes.

"Is this a joke?"

His laugh was loud as it echoed off the wall, causing the curtains behind me to sway a little. No human could do that. "Come on, Carly doll. I expected a hug," he said.

Slowly, I moved for my purse, which I'd thrown onto the couch earlier. I suddenly had the energy to not only drive back down that hill but also to head back into Indianapolis again. My mother's basement awaited me. I cringed thinking about it, mostly because I'd made a "this is my life" speech about independence and never coming back that might've included something about a septic tank. Why did I have to burn every bridge?

I took a step back then another, never taking my eyes off the strange, yet familiar, figure floating in the shadows.

"Leaving so soon? But you just got here."

I must be imagining this, I told myself. "Ghosts aren't real," I said out loud in an almost defiant tone.

"Yet here we are." He crossed his arms so I could see the dumb elbow patches better. So I would know for sure it was him. He went on. "I have to say, I'd forgotten how cute you are when you're caught off guard."

I threw my purse back down on the couch. "I should've known this would be the reason you'd give me a house. You somehow knew you'd be able to come back and haunt it, so you thought it'd be fun to make Carly's life miserable one more time around. Well, I don't need to stay here."

That was a lie. I did. My mother said she'd be charging more rent if I came back.

He disappeared from the doorway, reappearing right next to me, and I screamed.

"I'm here because I need your help. I didn't mean to scare you. I do hope I didn't scare you."

I shook my head. "Nope, just annoyed me, like always." I was mostly annoyed I needed to get in touch with the lawyer and tell him to give this place to the Bowmans or Destiny, or whoever was next in line; I didn't care.

"Caaaarrrrllllly Mae!" Someone called from the veranda door off my kitchen.

I didn't move. For some strange reason, I was no longer sure if it was a human voice or another ghost's. Jackson disappeared and I slowly walked toward it.

"Caaaarly Mae!"

"It's just Carly now." I peeked out the kitchen window and almost toppled over. All I could see was a tuft of light blonde hair and the kind of broad shoulders that made little old ladies lose their bladder control. I knew exactly who it was.

"Brock Calhoun," I said, my lungs finally able to breathe normally.

He looked through the window at me with that same wild boyish grin from when we were younger, and I almost lost my faculties too. He looked good, but the best part was I could finally admit how good he looked now that I was a single lady, and he was a single man.

I threw the door open and hugged him, surprised by how strong he was when he lifted me up a little. He smelled good, like cologne. Single men always did. It was only after you married them that you got to smell their true selves, "Eau de no longer trying."

"Old George told me you were up at Gate House. So I wanted to come by, see if you needed anything." He held up a bag from Thriftway. "I brought you a frozen pizza. I remember you used to love those things."

I snatched the bag from his hand like a hungry animal and looked inside. There was also beer.

"Bless you," I said, my eyes almost tearing up.

He continued. "I would've called, but I won't have your phone number until tomorrow," he said, looking me over.

I felt my face growing hot. "How will you have my number tomorrow? I mean, I'll give it to you, if you want it. Do you want it? The phone company's coming at eleven. But you can have my cell phone number right now." Tina's face came to my mind, and the guilt that went with it.

This was her man.

He pulled on the name-tag part of his light blue button down shirt that bulged at the seams in all the right places. At first I only noticed the shirt, but then I saw what he was getting at. He was holding his name tag. "I forgot you worked for Landover Cable and Phone," I said, turning on the oven and tossing the pizza onto a cold rack. I turned back around. He was staring at me.

"You look good," he said, without hesitation, like he wasn't just politely lying. I knew my frizz was extra frizzy, probably lumping out of its bun in a clown-like poof. I smoothed my hand over it to check. It wasn't too bad. I'd sneak off in a minute to check a mirror.

Brock Calhoun was voted sexiest man at the Thriftway by the girls there way back when. There were really only three of us voting. And after he asked Tina out instead of me, I changed my vote.

"Need some help moving in?" he asked. "Or do you like your car being full of stuff?"

"I'm not staying," I admitted.

His face dropped. "Really? Why?"

"Maybe I'll stay. I don't know." *Had I really just said that?*

Was I seriously thinking about staying in a creepy old house that my annoying ex-husband was in the middle of haunting in a town with a murderer on the loose because a cute boy seemed interested? Being 31 and single had made me significantly more desperate than I ever thought I'd be. "I think the place might be haunted."

I pulled open the top drawer on the kitchen island and grabbed the bottle opener that I knew would be in there because it was always in there. I opened one of the beers and handed it to him. He took it and handed me something long and dangly back. It was a silver necklace with a shiny black stone pendant.

"Obsidian," he said, matter-of-factly, like that meant something. "My aunt thinks this place is haunted. It's from her."

His aunt Rosalie owned an upscale hippie shop in the main part of Potter Grove that sold overpriced incense and beaded clothing. I also heard she did seances and read people's cards on the weekends to make a little extra cash. None of the rich baby-boomer ex-hippies who vacationed at Landover Lake could leave the area without stopping in at Rosalie's Purple Pony shop. He pointed to the stone. "It's supposed to ward off evil spirits, if you believe in that stuff."

I couldn't put the necklace on fast enough. "So this gets rid of spirits, huh? Evil ones," I said loudly so my ex would hear me. "They won't be able to touch me? Or follow me around? Or talk to me at all," I asked.

"Are they doing that right now?" Brock's horrified expression let me know I shouldn't answer that truthfully.

"Come on," I said, taking another swig off my beer. "Let's go get my stuff. I guess I'll give this place a trial period." Again, I seemed to mostly be talking to my ex.

There were three levels to the main part of the house. The

second floor had zero options for me to sleep in, unless I wanted to sleep in the nursery (with the bug-eyed weird horse sculpture mounted on the wall that I seriously doubted any living child actually picked out) or the maid's quarters down the hall from it. Nope. I pointed up the staircase to the man who was carrying the boxes. Sweat dripped from Brock's temple.

"You sure you don't want help?" I asked.

He shook his head "no," and we kept going up. Since I wasn't about to stay in the master, my only other options were a creepy room with what looked like dead blackbirds pasted to the wall or the room I'd begun calling *Old Lady Death* because its fleur-de-lis patterned wallpaper looked like a dead grandmother's dress. I pointed to Old Lady Death.

"I bet you start remodeling right away," Brock said when he saw the room. He set the suitcases on the bed and sat down on the wooden chair off to the side that looked more like an electric chair than one made for comfort.

"I wish I could. I signed an agreement not to touch anything in the house."

He laughed, but when I didn't laugh with him, he stopped. "You're serious."

"Part of the trial basis," I said. "I'm not sure I can live in a horror house."

"Sorry." He looked around, like he was searching for something to compliment. "Wallpaper's nice."

"Yes, if you like the lining of a casket. I'll probably spend most of my time terrified, but at least I'll have Rex."

"Rex is good protection," he said, looking over at the dog who had peeked into the room as if on cue. "But he's an old dog. You should get a gun or some mace. You heard about the..."

I nodded. "Murders? Another reason this is a trial arrangement. I'm not sure I want to live in a place where I have no cellphone coverage, and I need a gun or mace."

"Or a strong man for protection."

I shoved my hands in my pocket and gulped. I knew my face was getting red. "Pizza's probably done," I said, turning back down the hall.

Brock bent down and picked up a long gray rock from off the red carpeting. "You dropped something," he said, handing it to me.

I checked my pocket. It must've been the thing Rex had given me before. I held it up to the window at the end of the hall where a little bit of light was struggling to make it around the heavy curtains. "Rex brought this to me when I was talking to the lawyer. What do you think it is?"

"I don't know," Brock said, taking it from my hand. "Sure looks like a bone to me."

CHAPTER 4

A FAVOR

"You don't think this bone is human, do you?" I asked as I chugged my beer by the kitchen island downstairs.

He shrugged. "Could be."

"Then I'm going to take it to the sheriff first thing tomorrow. But tonight, I'm going to board up the entire house and sleep snuggled up with that block of steak knives as my pillow."

Brock snapped a picture of the bone with his cellphone. "Wait, you're gonna take this bone to the sheriff tomorrow? Really? To Sheriff Caleb Bowman?" He raised his beer to his lips but chuckled so hard he almost spilled it. "You two buddy-buddy now that you got the house he always thought he should own?"

"Shoot. I forgot Caleb was the sheriff." Caleb was Jackson's cousin, and the person most people thought should've been next in line for the inheritance since Jackson hadn't had any children. I took a bite of pizza. It burned the roof of my mouth. "I'll take the bone to Justin then," I mumbled with my mouth full of burning hot pizza. Justin was the deputy. He was also my ex. So, my choices for turning in the bone were: awkward sheriff or slightly less awkward deputy. *Welcome back to Potter Grove, Carly.*

Brock leaned into me, both of us standing pretty close at the kitchen island while we ate our pizza straight off the cooling rack, looking out the window without saying too much. I felt the warmth of his hand getting closer to mine. As soon as our fingers touched, a thunderous jolt shook the house. We both turned around. Brock had pizza smeared across the front of his shirt. The sound of cicadas picked up outside, like laughter. Then a cookbook fell off the top shelf of the kitchen cabinet, almost smacking him square on the head.

"What the hell?" he shouted. "An earthquake?"

I grabbed my necklace and glared around the room at nothing.

"Here, let me help you clean up," I said, yanking open the dish towel drawer, watching the room for more flying stuff.

"Don't worry about it. I should get going, anyway, unless you're afraid."

"No, I'm fine. I have Rex. Besides, I don't want you to have to drive down in the dark. It took me almost half an hour to get up that hill today."

He laughed. "I've got a truck, Carly Mae. I'll be down in ten-fifteen minutes, tops. But you should really get the drive paved. Backside of the hill too. It could be a shortcut into Landover from this side of Potter Grove. You know that right?"

I nodded. I did know that. It had been a sore spot between me and Jackson when we were living here and commuting into Landover, which meant a long drive down the hill and back around when all we really had to do was pave the back of the hill.

"Yeah, there are a bunch of things I wish I could change around here," I said. I watched him leave. His slightly tight, dark blue work pants looked good from all angles, even with a pair of latex work gloves sticking out of his back pocket, swishing around like a bright blue tail.

I did like a guy in uniform.

My stomach turned, thinking about Tina, the guilt building up along with the resentment that I was basically second fiddle over here with Brock.

I wondered how my old friend was doing, if she was finally out of her "rough patch," which was what Mrs. Carmichael called her schizophrenia.

Hearing Brock's truck maneuvering its way over the rocks as he pulled out of the driveway sent a chill up my spine. I was alone again.

I picked up the cookbook that had fallen off the top shelf. A photo bookmarked one of the pages, so I opened to it. It was a picture of me and Jackson back when we were dating. I had flour on my face from my failed attempt at tossing pizza dough, and he was laughing at me. I ran my finger over the photo. We had some good times back before he turned into a controlling, drunken stripper-lover.

"He's not very bright, you know?"

It was my ex again. I slowly ran my hand down my face. "Who are you talking about, Jackson? Brock? Maybe he's just not very arrogant and stuck on himself so that's what's throwing you off."

"No, the man's a walking drool cup."

Just like when we were married, I ignored him and

grabbed a Ziploc bag from a drawer and began putting pizza in it.

He leaned against the cabinet as he talked, like a ghost could get comfortable. "The guy feels the kitchen island hit him in the back, a cookbook flies off the shelf, and pizza is smeared on the front of his work shirt, and all he can do is grunt and say, 'Me go home?' Your knight in shining armor. Congratulations. He's a keeper."

"Shut up," I said. "You do not get to talk to me, at all. Ever. You know what? When you gave me this house, I thought, *'Maybe Jackson wasn't that bad after all, Carly. Sure, he cheated on you with Destiny and left you with nothing but bills and regret, but maybe there was some sort of kindness there.'* I was wrong."

I chucked the bag of pizza across the room at him. It flew right through his stomach like nothing was there. I ran up the first flight of stairs, unclasping the stupid obsidian necklace as I ran. It obviously did nothing to ward off evil.

He hovered right behind me. "Like I was saying before we were interrupted by Sir Drools-a-lot back there, I need your help."

I ran up the second flight of stairs, my breath growing heavy as I did. This was going to be a lot of work, running away from my 50-something-year-old, immature ghost of an ex who no longer seemed to tire. "Why in the hell should I help you," I asked, trying not to sound out of breath.

"I will leave if you'll do me one favor."

I stopped and turned toward him, surprised by how life-like and sad his eyes looked at the moment. "So you're saying you'll leave forever?"

He put his head down like he was hurt by that. "If you want."

"Yes, done. What is it?"

"I want you to solve my murder."

I rolled my eyes. "That is going to be very hard to do. I heard you died of a heart attack. Drinking and strippers will do that to a man in his fifties."

He patted the area that used to contain his heart, not that I thought he ever had one. "You looked up the cause of my death? You do care."

"Nope."

"Did it ever occur to you that it was ruled a heart attack because the coroner was in on it?"

I closed my eyes and tried to will him to leave. I opened my eyes again. He was still there. "Not everything has a conspiracy theory behind it. I seriously doubt your heart attack was made up by a diabolical coroner."

"Suspicious things started happening to me just before I died. Someone cut the brakes on my car. Another time, I spent all night in the emergency room. Hospital staff couldn't figure it out, but I knew I'd been poisoned. I even filled out a report with Caleb. At the time, I thought Destiny was involved. But after the police did nothing about it, I thought Caleb might've been. All I knew was the attempts on my life had to be tied to my will, so I cut a few key players out. My cousins, my uncle, my wife."

"And you gave the house to me."

"The one person who loved me for me and would actually take care of Rex."

"I'll look into your death, but you also have to promise to butt out of my personal life," I said. "No more throwing cookbooks or smearing pizzas. No more calling Brock Sir Drools-a-lot. Hopefully, you'll be seeing a lot of him."

"I can hardly wait. He's very charming. Drool and all. So, it's a deal?"

"Sure," I replied. "But what if I find out you died of natural causes?"

His voice was right up next to me now, whispering. "I didn't, but if that's your conclusion after what I deem to be a thorough investigation then, sure. I'll move on."

I wasn't really going to look into his death. My ex was crazy. The only person who wanted to see him dead was the person he was dumb enough to give his house to, or was dumb enough to take it. I wasn't sure which one of us was Sir Drools-a-lot yet.

"One other thing," I said before he faded away. "If you see anything suspicious..."

"You mean like a murderer?"

"Yes. Feel free to wake me up or scare them off."

Now that I knew what was haunting this house, I wasn't afraid anymore, just pissed off I had to live with it.

I moved my stuff to the master bedroom as soon as I got upstairs, surprised by how easy it was to make the move, and how empowered I felt making it. I set my suitcase down on the large king-sized four-poster with the crisp white quilt and watched it sink into the lumpy mattress. The last time I'd been up here, more than four years ago, Jackson and Destiny were laying side by side in this very bed. They hadn't even bothered to lock the door. Jackson knew the precise moment I got home from the university every single day, too. Tuesdays was 7:46, right after I taught the 101 English class as a graduate assistant. He must've wanted me to find them.

Thinking back on how Rex had greeted me downstairs that night, I can see it was more like a warning the way he tugged on the hem of my favorite cigarette pants not allowing me to go up the stairs. I should've known something was up. Jackson had been acting differently for months, along with everyone else around me too. The hushed whispers of the other staff members at Landover University when they'd notice me walking by. Everyone knew Carly Mae's husband had been going to the strip clubs, drunk and disorderly, hanging over all the women.

But I blocked it out, dismissed it as a midlife crisis. I'd even checked out a book on how to help someone through such a weird part of their life. *So he liked a little porn?* A lot of men did. It wasn't like he was cheating on me.

I was carrying that stupid library book when I heard giggling coming from the other side of my bedroom door.

Funny how I remember the very outfit I was wearing and the book I was carrying. The book I should've thrown at them, and would have if I hadn't remembered last second that it was a library book. I was never going to let myself forget even one painful moment or detail from that night because I knew in the back of my mind that remembering it was the only way I was never going to repeat it.

I had a backbone now. I was no longer sweet, stupid Carly Mae, the girl who was last to know about her husband's affair. I was Carly.

And this man was no longer welcome in my house. Not even dead.

CHAPTER 5

I could feel the small-town gossip already forming as I drove through town the next day. People noticing my car, elbowing the person they were walking with while mouthing the words, "That's her." They all knew so much about me, and Jackson, and Destiny, and the Bowmans — the main reason I left in the first place.

Today, with my shiny new lipgloss (thanks to Shelby) and my hot pink sundress that was probably about four inches too short for most people in town even though it was knee level, I waved back to them. "That's right. The girl who refuses to buy a truck even though she could probably use one isn't Carly Mae anymore," I said to the town as I passed them. "She's just Carly now... even if she hasn't been able to correct anyone on that name change yet."

The Purple Pony was a little shop crying out for attention, and it had no problems getting it in this beige town. A gigantic, glittery, wooden, purple and yellow unicorn smiled at patrons as they entered from the top of the door. I used to go here more often than I needed to (because who needs to go to a hippie shop that often) for the same reason everyone else did. Its owner, Rosalie Cooper. You weren't someone unless you had a crazy "Rosalie story" or two to swap around town.

When I entered, I wasn't the least bit surprised to find it empty. It was a 50-50 shot you'd get any customer service at the Purple Pony. Rosalie was usually in the back making jewelry or painting something colorful.

While the outside of the store was bright and loud, the inside was its equal in quiet and subdued, mostly earth tones, with brown Oriental rugs and plants interspersed among the racks of mostly tan, but beaded and adorned, shirts and skirts.

"I'm in the back," she yelled when she heard the wind chimes on the door. I walked through the maze of incense smells into the back room. Rosalie was behind a large easel, her thick bare arms moving in wild strokes like a mad woman as she dabbed on a brush of turquoise, a glob of silver. I hugged her from behind, avoiding the still-wet-looking blue paint streaks spiraling around a dreadlock, and thanked her for the necklace. She almost fell over.

"What do you think?" she asked, motioning toward the colorful lion in front of her. Her eyes, which were the same color as the paint in her hair, really stood out behind her almost nonexistent eyelashes. She never wore makeup and didn't need to.

"It's going to fit in perfectly."

She leaned back and stared at it a second. "Needs more yellow."

"Lions tend to be yellow," I said.

She nodded, and reached her brush into the little glob of yellow on her palette, brushing it gingerly along the sides of its green mane. "You know, when I heard you were here, I told Brock he needed to go up there with that necklace. I tell you,

Carly Mae, there's something evil about that house you inherited..."

"Yes," I told her. "My ex-husband."

She laughed like I was joking. Her long gray dread-locked ponytail bounced from one shoulder to the next.

I lowered my voice and told her everything that had happened yesterday, minus the part about how Jackson thought her nephew was dumb. Rosalie was the only person I could mention these things to, the only person who'd believe me if I told her I had a ghost.

She cocked her head to the side and her mouth fell open a little. "So, you're saying you had an actual, voices-heard conversation with your dead ex-husband?"

I nodded. Maybe I was wrong to think she'd believe me. "He thinks he was murdered, and he wants me to investigate it for him."

She went back to her painting. "I thought he had a heart attack?"

"He did. He was pretty delusional when he was alive, too."

She wiped her fingers on her smock and scooted her stool over to the sky blue and purple antique cabinet sitting along one of the back walls. "I think I know why you inherited that house," she said, yanking on a semi-stuck drawer. It finally opened and she pulled out a small heart-shaped plastic device that looked like it came out of a Ouija board game. "This is a planchette. It's how most people talk to the deceased. I don't use it, but a lot of mediums do. They ask the spirit-world questions and it uses their hands to write down answers. But you're saying you've got direct-voice mediumship."

"Yeah. But I could definitely see him too."

"Holy smokes. If I'd have known you had such a gift, I would've hired you to do seances with me."

"I never had anything like this happen to me before," I said, trying to think back in my life to make sure that was true. I used to have invisible friends back when I was little that seemed pretty real. But then, that was mostly because I was not a popular kid.

"It's like any gift. You have to practice it in order to get control over it. I wonder if that's why they left you the house," Rosalie said, nodding.

"They?"

"The Bowmans."

"The Bowmans?" I chuckled. "The Bowmans didn't leave me squat. Jackson Bowman did."

"I wasn't talking about the living Bowmans, dear. I was talking about the ones at Gate House. We should do a seance there."

I shook my head, "no." Something told me the house would hate that. It was probably written in blood somewhere in my 75-page contract. "I just want to get rid of my ex-husband, that's all," I said. "I can't get dressed, thinking he's watching me. I can hardly go to the bathroom. And he's crazy. He threw a cookbook at Brock last evening because, get this, I think he was jealous."

She fell right into my trap. She threw me a knowing smile. "He's single, you know, and handsome. But then I'm probably biased; 6 foot 3, blue eyes, single. Did I mention the single part?"

I blushed. "So he and Tina are through then? For good?"

"Yeah, they haven't been a couple for more than a year. He did all he could on that one, more than most. She has to be the one to take her pills and try to get better."

It sounded like Tina's schizophrenia was still getting the best of her after four years of treatment.

Rosalie pulled out a small, dark green, worn-out book from the same drawer as the planchette. The book was old and its pages seemed to crackle and stick together as she thumbed through them. She stopped somewhere in the middle and pointed to a passage. "Ah, here it is. Sometimes spirits may not realize their presence is inappropriate..."

"I'm pretty sure this one does," I said. "I think he's trying to be inappropriate."

"Even if he knows, there are still ways to encourage him to move on to a higher life."

"Or a lower one," I chuckled. "Whichever side will take him."

Rosalie ignored my joke and continued. "But in the case of that house, I think there might be a deeper disturbance going on there, maybe a curse," she said. "Or, at least, that's been the rumor for a while. I can come over and try a few things tomorrow morning before I open shop, if you want. I've been wanting a shot at Gate House since I was a little girl. It's a clairvoyant's dream."

"Well then let's do it. Bring that book, and try everything in it," I said.

The wind chimes on the door rang again. Another customer. Rosalie slid off her stool and wobbled over to the main part of the store. I could tell her hip was bothering her again. That stubborn woman refused to carry a cane.

"Rosalie, is that Carly Mae's car out front?" a voice asked. I recognized it. Caleb Bowman, Jackson's cousin.

I came up behind Rosalie, peeking out from the corner of her shapeless green dress to see Caleb grinning at me in full sheriff uniform.

He looked older than I thought he'd look. It had only been four years since I'd seen him last, but he looked like he'd aged

15. He was younger than Jackson, but his pale, weathered face and dark brown goatee made him look like a sad commercial for beard dye.

He walked up closer to me, fixing his beady eyes on mine, like his stare and his police uniform were going to intimidate me.

"Enjoying my family's house?" he asked.

"It's okay, I guess. Little old."

This made his neck veins throb, and his teeth clench.

Rosalie stepped in front of us, her thick hands on her hips. She wobbled a little from her hip being unsteady and I grabbed one of her arms to help her. "Caleb, leave her alone," she said. "The only person you should be mad at is Jackson. Carly Mae had no idea your cousin was going to leave her that house. So why don't you go on down to the cemetery and spit on his grave or something useful like that."

He scratched at his bushy goatee with the back of his uniform-sleeved arm. "Come on, Rosalie. You know Jackson better than that. Would he have left his house to the ex-wife he obviously couldn't stand if he was in his right mind? That's gotta be a fake will or there's some nefarious reason. And I might know what that reason is. I just got done talking to my friends at the Landover police department. Everyone thinks it's weird how these murders and disappearances suddenly stopped the minute Jackson's heart did."

I looked at Rosalie then back at Caleb, trying not to look at my purse where I still had a suspicious bone in the compartment usually reserved for my cell phone.

Caleb went on. "You gonna pretend you don't know about the murders?"

"I was told when I came into town, but I don't know much."

"Well, go on down to the library and catch up on some local news." He looked at me about 10 seconds too long before leaving, as if not knowing enough about a murder somehow made you an accomplice to it. Potter Grove's finest, right there.

Rosalie turned to me. "It's just a rumor that's been making the rounds. You remember how small towns are."

I nodded. I was all too familiar.

"Jackson died about four months ago, around the same time the last strippers went missing. And no one's gone missing since. That's all. People talking nonsense. It's nothing."

"Strippers?" I said. No wonder they were accusing my ex. He did have a thing for strippers. And there was that bone in his yard... nobody but me knew that last part, though.

I still didn't think the bone in my purse could possibly have belonged to one of the missing women, though. Sure, my ex-husband had changed a lot over the years, and he did have a penchant for boozing it up with strippers. But murdering them and burying them in his backyard? That seemed like an awful lot of work for a privileged man who probably didn't even know if he owned a shovel. Besides, the ladies were only missing for four months. Even if they died on the first day, they wouldn't have been reduced to a skeleton yet. And this bone was about as clean as they got. I'd quietly turn it into Justin later.

But first I needed to learn more about these murders.

CHAPTER 6

STRIPPERS

*R*ight as you walk into the Landover County Library, on the back wall just above the copiers, hangs a gigantic black-and-white photo of the building's ribbon-cutting ceremony taken sometime in the 50s. Mrs. Nebitt, the town librarian, is the one holding the gigantic scissors. She was scowling then too.

I nodded my hello to her, but she barely peered up from behind the humungous computer monitor that hid all but the tiny glare from her coke bottle glasses and a tuft of cottony hair. Still, I thought she'd be happy to see me. Not too many people came into this library on a regular basis, but I had always been one of them. I waved. "Hi, Mrs. Nebitt. Remember me? It's Carly." I almost said "Carly Mae," only remembering at the last second to leave the Mae part off. She grunted out an irritated shushing noise. *Aww*, she did remember me.

Twelve years ago, when I first walked into this library and signed up for a library card, she'd given me that same disapproving look, like I had been trying to obtain a fake ID or something. Cheat the town out of a whole slew of funny-smelling paperbacks. Then, after finding out I was about to be Jackson Bowman's wife, she made a point of telling me what she thought of that.

"Tell me something," she said, over-enunciating each syllable. "What kind of a young lady marries her much older professor? And what kind of a man does she get? A decent one?" I thought at the time that she was just bitter and mean, and that she should mind her own business and stop talking in cryptic riddles. And now, her scowl was extra smug. She'd been right.

I grabbed a stack of Gazettes and sat down with them at the one rectangular table in the periodicals section right next to an extra-large "Quiet" sign. My chair made a screeching sound across the tile and Mrs. Nebitt shushed me again, even though we were the only two in the library. Apparently, decent people worked on Thursday mornings, and everyone else should be scolded for drawing attention to their squeaky chairs and lack of employment.

Every single Landover Gazette had a story about the murders and the missing women. No wonder Caleb thought it was suspicious that I hadn't heard much about them. They'd been the talk of the town for some time. He didn't realize there was a lot of news like this in Indianapolis. So much so, we hardly needed to get more of it from other cities.

The girls ranged in age from 18 to 24, all were nude dancers, two had lived in Potter Grove, two from Landover. I started at the beginning with an article titled, *Police Still Baffled By Missing Women*. I thought about the police here in Potter Grove. That sounded about right.

Trish Jenkins, 24, and Kelly Moore, 23, were last seen at work at the

Night Owl in Landover on October 31 and were reported missing three days later by their parents after not returning calls or texts. Police do not suspect foul play at this time. Sources say the women were roommates behind on their rent and known to leave town for various questionable parties, sometimes not returning for days.

I scanned through the pile of nothing-new articles until I found the next interesting one, the date their bodies were discovered. March 4.

Local Boy Scouts Make Gruesome Discovery

While collecting trash along Main Street Saturday morning, Boy Scout Troop 9071 at first thought they'd found a wig sticking out of the dirt. Upon further investigation it was determined to be human remains. Police were summoned immediately. No confirmation has been made on the identities of the victims, but they are believed to be those of missing Landover dancers, Trish Jenkins and Kelly Moore.

The strangest part was that they were found without clothes or fingers. Police later discovered the fingers, stripped of flesh straight down to the bones, in a Ziploc bag next to the bodies.

I wondered if they were the same Ziploc bags I had frozen pizza in right now. I couldn't stop reading between the lines that the bone in my purse was probably connected to these women.

Apparently, the still-missing women were the younger of the bunch. One was just about to turn 19 when she went missing in March. She was stripping her way through college at Landover University, and her parents were particularly distraught in one of the interviews, blaming themselves because they couldn't afford her education, begging for her safe return. She was an English major who always wore a large blue pendant necklace her parents gave her when she started college. It had a Shakespearean quote engraved on the back: *We know what we are, but not what we may be.*

I felt my shoulders hunching as I read. I had been 19 when I took Jackson's class. I was an English major too. Had she been one of his pupils? I couldn't help but notice the woman had similarities to both me and Jackson's second wife, Destiny.

Whoever wrote the article made it seem like these women had it coming to them. "Seen around town in scantily clad dresses, inviting perversion."

Inviting perversion?

I realized I was clenching my teeth and I tried to relax. I used to blame Destiny for Jackson cheating on me, like her "scantily clad clothes" had invited his perversion. Truth was, he was the one who caused his own perversion. He was the problem. I almost wished he was also a murderer. Then, I'd have another reason to hate him. Then, the threat would be over for any more women. But, I honestly didn't think he could have done this.

I gathered up the Gazettes and carefully put them away so I wouldn't get an extra scowl. Then I grabbed my purse to head down to the station.

"I knew you'd come in here." It was Caleb Bowman's booming voice, yelling from across the library. Mrs. Nebitt didn't even shush him. "Did you find some evidence at *your* house that you're looking up? Is that the reason my cousin gave you everything? Because he knew you'd be the one person who'd cover up a murder for him?"

I whisper-yelled back to him. "You are really grasping at straws here, Caleb, and we both know it. Nobody plans things out like that, and besides, I would be the last person to help that man out, dead or alive."

"You might for a free house and a significant inheritance."

Mrs. Nebitt shushed me. *Me.* Even though Caleb had been yelling the entire time.

I lowered my voice even lower. "You'll stop at nothing to try to take that inheritance, though, huh?"

There was no way he could have known I had discovered evidence at my house unless he planted that evidence, if it was evidence, which it probably wasn't.

I pushed by him and went straight to the police station, only because I knew Caleb wouldn't be there. And I could trust the deputy. Maybe.

Christine, a middle-aged woman with short red hair, thick cheeks, and a wide smile, rushed over as soon as I stepped through the door. "Carly Mae. I heard you were back in town."

I gave her a quick hug. Justin and Christine both seemed normal. I had no idea how they put up with a spastic man-child like Caleb day after day. "Is Justin here?"

"No, he's out on patrol. Why?"

I briefly thought about giving her the evidence, but I wasn't sure it was even evidence or what was going on. "Can I leave you my number to have him call me?"

"Sure. Why? He's single, you know? And just as cute as ever."

I was starting to notice you couldn't be a single woman in Potter Grove without people trying to throw men at you. I wondered briefly why I left.

When I didn't say anything, Christine's smile fell. "That's right. I forgot you two dated." She quickly looked down at her paperwork again, making me realize my reputation around this place might be tainted by whatever stories Justin Fortworth was telling everyone.

I scribbled my number and a quick "Call me as soon as you get this" note on the sticky note she handed me, debating for a good half a minute whether I should add that it was about business so he wouldn't think something else. I didn't.

Then I hightailed it over to the Walmart to pick up some food for the house and the ugliest swimsuit I could find to shower in. I did not trust my awful, perverted dead ex-husband to know his boundaries at my house. He was, after all, still the problem.

But before Rosalie got rid of him tomorrow, he had some explaining to do, about bones in the yard and possible missing strippers.

CHAPTER 7

ON SHAKY GROUND

*B*rock's large white work truck was already waiting for me when I got up the hill to Gate House. He was right on time. In more ways than one, I was pretty sure.

He looked exactly the same as yesterday -- same blue uniform and work pants -- but when he got out of his truck, my mouth dropped. I'd forgotten how good exactly-the-same could look sometimes. I adjusted my curls and sucked in my stomach before getting out of my car. The humidity instantly smacked my face and threatened my hair again. Rats. I was going to look exactly the same too.

"You look good," he said, making me happy I'd taken the time to touch up my lip gloss while heading up the hill.

He grabbed two of the bags from my grasp, and I made sure neither had the awful grandma swimsuit in it that I bought for wearing around my ex, something I still couldn't believe I had to do. Not for long. Rosalie was coming tomorrow, I reminded myself.

As we made our way to the veranda, I squinted at the patio table and chairs. They seemed to be shaking a little. The small potted plant on the side of the kitchen door jiggled like it was doing a dance then fell over.

Slowly, I put my foot on the first step up to the porch. An almost shocking vibration ran up my leg, making my veins itch. I pulled it off again. The veranda was shaking, all right. It had to be my dead ex-husband. I couldn't wait to get rid of that guy.

Was he going to be like this every time people came over?

Brock was about to step onto the veranda when the front door swung open and a cloud of dust almost smacked us in the face. All I could see was a swiftly moving broom, but I knew who was holding it. Mrs. Harpton. I'd forgotten she always came on Thursdays. I'd only met the woman two other times. Jackson used to say she was the only housekeeper the Bowman family trusted with the Victorian.

But I always avoided the strange woman when I was married, which was just fine with Mrs. Harpton. She liked to do her cleaning and managing of the property without anyone around. According to her, "People slowed her."

Her long, heavy, black dress scratched along the veranda as she moved. Her dark hair was always severely parted in the middle and plastered to her head in lumpy waves that seemed to poof out at the bottom and tuck into themselves.

When she saw us approaching, she curved her mouth farther down into its folds and shooed us away with the broom. "Not done yet," she said in lieu of a smile. Her voice quivered as she spoke. "Come back in 20 minutes."

I stepped onto the shaky veranda. "We won't get in your way," I said. "I promise. But we do need to get into the house. We have to set up the phone and cable."

"Don't care," she said, briskly spinning about with her broom. She looked like a stiff dark blur with movements that were both fluid and mechanical at the same time. "Phone and cable were supposed to come at 11:00, but you changed the appointment."

"Yes," I said. "I changed it because I was busy at eleven."

"Be done in 20 minutes. Come back then," she said, shutting the door behind her.

I looked back at Brock, who seemed to be laughing a little under his breath.

"I think she's using some kind of machine or something that's shaking the house. It's probably best if we just wait the twenty minutes."

We put the bags back in my car and Brock suggested we go for a walk around the outside of my house, something I didn't exactly want to do. I was wearing my good sandals and the outside of the house was mostly just overgrown bushes and trees, lots of places to catch Lyme Disease or find the dead strippers your husband killed.

The cicadas picked up as we made our way around the wooded area. Sweat dripped along the back of my neck, and I briefly thought about going back to the car to get a beer, but Brock probably couldn't drink on the job, and it wouldn't be polite to drink in front of him.

Every once in a while, he'd look over at me and smile, the side of his face growing red. "Don't tell Tina, but back when we were all working at Thriftway, I was going to ask you out first."

I smiled, remembering those days. It seemed like ages ago. "Things probably would've been a lot different if you had," I admitted, immediately kicking myself for saying something so telling. Truth was, I wasn't sure I believed him right now. He was probably saying what he thought a second fiddle wanted to hear, when first fiddle was no longer an option.

Everyone thought Brock and Tina were going to get married. They'd been dating on and off again for forever. Then, Tina had her first "rough spell" about four years ago. One day the poor girl seemed fine and the next, she was freaking out at the Shop-Quik, yelling that grizzly bears with blue-shoveled claws were conspiring with her mother to bite all of her limbs off, eat them like hotdogs.

I was just about to ask Brock about Tina when he stopped walking. "I always wanted to know something about you."

I stopped and looked at him, his blue eyes seemed to almost sparkle in the sunlight.

"Why'd you marry Jackson? He was so old." He paused. He looked down at his work boots then back up again.

Great. The rumor was back again. Everyone, including the town librarian, thought I dumped Justin for the obvious reasons.

"His money," I said because the question took me by surprise, and it had been rude.

He chuckled. "I heard it was daddy issues. You didn't grow up with a dad."

"Neither did you," I shot back then thought better about it. I stared at him, not sure how to correct my snippiness, not sure I wanted to. It was something Brock and I had in common. I knew Rosalie's sister adopted him, right before her husband died. We both only had adopted moms growing up.

Mine had a slightly different story, though. My mother was one of those power-suit-wearing 80s-ladies who pummeled through glass ceilings with her shoulder pads. First woman engineer at Stellaplex in 1975. First woman supervisor by '83. But sometime along the way, in her early 40s, she looked around and realized she'd forgotten to have kids. So she took the next logical step and adopted. She didn't need a man in the picture. And we never had one.

I shrugged. "It doesn't matter, anyway," I said. "Things were good with Jackson until they weren't. But he wasn't like a dad. He was someone I could trust who protected me. Sure, he told corny jokes, but he gave pretty good advice and... oh god, maybe there were some daddy issues in there."

He slipped his hand into mine and turned toward me. I felt myself holding my breath. "We should get dinner sometime and really catch up on things," he said, looking first at the forest then up at the sky. He seemed to be avoiding my eyes.

I pulled my hand away. I wasn't sure how dating him would go over in a town that was probably still rooting for Tina. I knew I should be rooting for her too. Realizing I was hesitating too long and Brock was still staring at the sky, I quickly said, "Yes." I couldn't let the collective feelings of a gossipy town affect my happiness.

A real friend would contact Tina. A real friend would ask her how she felt about things.

The ground shook under our feet like something large was rumbling nearby. I could tell some sort of large vehicle was making its way up my drive.

"Expecting someone?" he asked.

"Only Mrs. Harpton," I replied as we slowly walked toward the sound. A cloud of dust gave way to a black and white SUV police car. Caleb Bowman's smirk gleamed through the front windshield.

He rolled down his window and shoved a piece of paper into the air as he hit the last bumps of my driveway. The paper flapped wildly like it was waving *hello*.

"Search warrant," he yelled.

CHAPTER 8

WHAT REMAINS TO BE SEEN

*P*ride wouldn't let me walk faster than a slow stroll over to the man's police car. Plus, Justin was in there with him.

And damn it, he looked good. His thick dark hair blew in the wind from his open window, and I could only catch a glimpse of his almond-shaped eyes before he saw me looking at him and looked away. His short-sleeved uniform showed off his muscular arms covered in the kinds of tattoos my mother would spend the rest of her days googling if she ever saw them, convinced they were gang related.

"Sorry to bother you, Carly Mae," Justin said in a strictly business tone as I approached the SUV. "Let's hope this is nothing."

"I'm sure it is, knowing the source here," I said, directing my remark to Caleb. I snatched the paper from him and examined it. It mentioned me and the fact I had found a possible human bone... "What? How on earth?"

Justin got out of the car and bro-embraced Brock while

the sheriff fumbled around on his phone. After a short second, Caleb handed the phone to me, and my attention went to the picture on his screen. It was the one Brock had taken yesterday while we were drinking beer.

Brock came around to the other side of the car and glanced over my shoulder. "Oh yeah, I sent that to Justin."

"After he showed it around the Spoony River last night, asking if it could be one of the strippers." Caleb added.

My ex-husband's words echoed through my head. "*He's not very bright, you know...*"

"I only wonder why you didn't turn that in," Caleb said to me, in a way that suggested there was a huge conspiracy behind my actions. The Bowmans liked their conspiracy theories.

I pulled the Ziploc out of my purse and handed it to Caleb like it was no big deal. "I didn't think it was a bone, but I left a message for Justin about it earlier today."

No wonder Caleb had been so smug at the library earlier. He probably already had the wheels in motion for that search warrant, the cartoon-villain jerk. "You could just have asked me about it. Asked to search the property. You didn't need a warrant."

"A professional canine unit will be arriving here any minute... from Landover," he said, like that was something impressive. I shrugged and went to get my Walmart bags from my car, slowly making my way into the house, even though I wasn't sure Mrs. Harpton was done and that I'd even be able to get in there yet.

Thankfully, the door swung open to a spotless kitchen. Mrs. Harpton had some skills; the woman was fast and efficient, and the place never smelled like harsh chemicals when she was done or anything. "Mrs. Harpton," I half-yelled into the house when I entered through the kitchen, hoping she wouldn't actually hear me. I didn't want her shooing me out the door again.

The little pitter patter of dog claws sliding along the hardwood answered my yell. Rex couldn't get there fast enough.

"So, you don't mind if we have a look around?" Caleb asked, practically drooling over the house he thought should rightfully be his.

"Oh, I mind," I said. "But you have a search warrant, so unfortunately, that doesn't matter. But you may only check where your search warrant is valid for. I noticed right now that's just the woods and property outside Gate House." I shooed him back out the veranda door like I was Mrs. Harpton. Rex growled at him, and I gave my dog an extra loving pat as the sheriff headed outside.

Justin and Brock had been buddies since kindergarten, and I could tell they were speaking some sort of unspoken language to each other. I wondered if Brock was somehow talking to him about dating me, like the way I should be talking to Tina.

"Did you get my note? I left it with Christine," I said to Justin, interrupting their eyebrow talk.

"I haven't been back to the station yet," he replied.

"Well, when you do, just know I was trying to turn the bone in." I mostly said that for Brock's benefit, so he'd know why I wanted my ex-boyfriend to call me.

Justin nodded, staring at me a second longer than I expected before heading out the kitchen door. Even though I'd dated the man for about four months before I dated Jackson, I didn't really know too much about him. No one did. He was one of those rare creatures in Potter Grove who didn't get talked about.

As soon as the door closed behind him, I leaned into Brock and lowered my voice. "I wish you wouldn't have shown that picture around last night."

"Sorry. I thought I was helping."

"It's just I know Caleb's looking for ways to get his hands on this house, and I want to be careful."

He had a bag full of cables in his hand. "I was honestly just trying to find out if anyone thought it was the missing girls The whole town's been on edge since the two women turned up murdered last year, with a bag of finger bones next to them. But you're right. This is an old house. That bone probably came from some family graveyard or something. And I should've let you handle it."

I nodded and he left to go install my cable.

I could hear Caleb yelling cuss words to Justin as they struggled with procedure. There weren't a lot of murders in Potter Grove, and they seemed to be googling what to do next.

I headed out onto the veranda when I heard the canine unit pulling up to my driveway. A brunette who looked more like a model than a police officer got out of the car along with a german shepherd. Caleb approached her. "You're Officer Grant?" he said, half-chuckling.

"Yes," she replied, stretching a pair of latex gloves over her fingers.

His face dropped. "I thought they said they were sending out professionals."

Justin backed away from the two as the woman's face sharpened.

"Excuse me?" she asked. "Sheriff Bowman, didn't this house

belong to your cousin?" She mumbled something into her radio. "I'm not sure I'm comfortable with you sitting in on this investigation."

The heat felt thicker, and I went back inside to grab a beer and some microwave popcorn. This was about to get good. Brock came in when the smell of butter filled the air.

"Poor Justin," he said, pulling off a disposable work glove so he could dig into the popcorn. "He hates that guy."

"Everybody hates that guy," I replied. I smiled a little to myself when the radioed orders must've included Caleb sitting in his police car while Justin and the woman left with the dog.

"Wait a second." I ran over to the glass cabinet in the dining room where antiques were displayed and grabbed the ridiculously old binoculars.

I could only see small glimpses of the woman and her dog as they left one trail and entered another, Justin following closely behind.

Suddenly, the dog took off down a trail and over into the woods, sniffing wildly, pacing back and forth. Justin and Officer Grant ran after him. I stuffed another huge handful of popcorn in my mouth, not even caring that I was shoveling my face like a starving, grunting animal. That's just the way I ate when I was nervous about something, and I couldn't take my eyes off the woods, praying that the dog had found a squirrel or an old buried pet turtle, or that he hadn't really smelled anything interesting. He was just excited to have so much open space.

I took the binoculars off and shoved them at Brock who was still watching by my side. I could only picture the parents from the article, pleading for the safe return of their daughter, blaming themselves because they couldn't afford to pay for the girl's education. And my ex-husband who seemed to have changed drastically during the last years of our marriage, along with the fact he sure liked strippers...

"Please let that be a squirrel," I muttered over and over again.

Officer Grant pushed her way through some overgrown bushes, emerging from the woods, and Caleb rushed over to her. She held a small plastic bag out to him that seemed to be glimmering in the sunlight.

"What is it?" I asked Brock.

He put the binoculars up to his eyes. "Ohmygod. It looks like a bag of bones. Maybe. I can't really tell. But there's a necklace with a large blue pendant in it," he replied.

I coughed on a popcorn kernel.

THE POLICE TAPED off most of my yard, and it didn't take but a couple minutes for more help to arrive. I couldn't watch the process even though it lasted all night long, the carefully bagging and photographing of the remains as uniformed and plain-clothed police officers hauled them into a van, professionals from all over Wisconsin, news crews too.

I hadn't even been able to listen to Brock when he tried to explain how my new remote worked for my TV or about my probably-going-to-be-spotty internet connection. "Look, Carly Mae," he finally said, after my fourteenth *Huh, what?* "You seem pretty shook up. Are you gonna be okay. I could stay here tonight. You know, on the couch."

Every part of me wanted to scream, "yes," and would have any other night. But, not tonight. I didn't want to see anyone or anything but my dead ex-husband.

Of course, I couldn't tell Brock that. After he left, I paced the floor, trying to figure out how to conjure up a ghost. If I had the ability to talk to ghosts, I needed to know how to summon them. I rubbed my temples and tried to concentrate. "Jackson," I said, whispering. I closed my eyes. "Jackson!" I repeated, a little louder that time into the dim lighting of my living room at dusk.

I blinked them open. A dark figure stood in the kitchen frame, leaning casually on the wall. A silhouette against the lights streaming from the many vehicles still parked out on the dirt lot that was my yard. "Jackson?" I asked just before my eyes adjusted and I realized it wasn't my ex. It was his cousin.

"Don't tell me you're going crazy like your friend, Tina Carmichael," he said. "I wouldn't doubt it, though. I hear trauma can bring out some real nut-job behavior, PTSD and all, and what could be more traumatic than knowing you were married to a murderer? That could've been you out there, half buried, with your fingers off... or did you know about that?"

"Okay, Caleb, did you need something? I'm really shook up, and I just want to go to bed."

"So you thought you'd stand in your living room and call out your dead ex-husband's name?"

"Please knock next time." My voice was weak, defeated almost.

He didn't seem to hear a word I was saying. "If you do talk to Jackson, tell him it looks like he's in a world of trouble."

"He's dead," I snapped. "I'm pretty sure he's received all the trouble he can get."

"Yes, burning in hell is probably pretty troublesome," Caleb's voice was smug and sing-songy. Jackson used to tell me there were two lines of the Bowman name. The church-going side. And the ones who had a shot at getting into heaven. Caleb was definitely the former.

He moved in closer to me. "I just came in to let the *home-owner* know we'll have people here all night, tomorrow too. Expect the FBI and probably the press as well. Sleep tight," he said. "You look good, Carly Mae." He headed out the door, and I locked and bolted it. Then I headed upstairs to try to summon the alleged murderer again.

CHAPTER 9

PLAYING FAVORITES

I slammed the door to my room and threw myself onto the bed, listening to the clinks and clanks of the workers outside, cleaning up what used to be life and vitality, reduced now to the regimen of paperwork and cleaning crews. The house agreement sat on the nightstand, a business envelope paper-clipped to it with my name on it. I opened the letter.

Dear Miss Taylor,

This letter serves as a formal written reprimand of your negligence in handling the property known as Gate House and its main living occupant, Rex, as inspected by Mrs. Theona Harpton. After three formal reprimands, appropriate actions can be expected. Please note the following areas of improvement...

There were more than one hundred areas of improvement, from how I was forbidden to change the schedule to how I couldn't leave plates on the drying rack past 10:00 at night.

I grabbed my phone and tried to jump on the internet. *I*

must have rights under this house agreement that Ronald failed to mention. I got nothing but a "cannot connect to internet" page.

I tossed the letter and my phone back on top of the agreement and let my head hit the pillow. I no longer wanted to confront my ex. I no longer cared. My mother's place in Indianapolis was looking better and better, even with her constant reminders that my eggs were on a timer. At least the internet would work and I'd have cell phone coverage. And no possibility of being murdered, at least not by anyone but family.

I could hear my mother's reaction. "Carly Mae, you have to stop quitting stuff when the going gets tough."

I turned over then jumped back when I saw Jackson's smug face laying next to me on my pillow. "I heard you call longingly for me downstairs."

"You heard wrong. I only want to know one thing, Jackson. Did you do it?" I could barely get the words out fast enough.

"Do what?"

"You know what. Kill those women the police are busy carrying away from our backyard."

I could hear the van doors slamming shut and the engines starting up, revving into the night. I checked his face for any signs that he'd known, that he was involved. His transparent appearance showed up better in the dim lighting of the one lamp I had in my room. But his expression never changed.

"Is that what all the fuss was about outside? As a new transformation, I only have enough energy to manifest myself in the one place I haunt, not outside of it yet. And it took a full day's rest to build up enough energy to do that. You're worth it, though."

"They think you did it," I said, almost half-whispering to

the ghost sitting beside me on the bed. "The Landover stripper murders."

"Sure, blame the dead guy... the only one who can't defend himself."

I looked at him. He was avoiding the question. "Did you do it?"

"No," he said. "I can't believe you need to ask me that. Not that it matters, but no. I didn't kill those women. I adore women. I could never hurt one."

"Physically."

He pushed his lip out in a mock-pouting way. "How many times do I have to apologize for that one?"

"Oh, I don't know. You could try once, but honestly, it doesn't matter," I said. He'd never apologized, for anything. Everything was my fault. Somehow, cheating on me with Destiny was my fault too.

He continued with his lie. "I hate myself for that. I have always loved you, from the moment I saw you staring intently at me from the front row of my English Lit class, your cute little three-ring binder already open and ready to take notes. You were so serious. I knew you were wise beyond your years..."

"Cut the crap," I said. Like most pretentious jerks, Jackson loved the sound of his own voice.

He got up from the bed and hovered by me, kneeling down a bit so our eyes could meet. He was a pretty tall hoverer. "I'm very sorry I cheated on you, Carly. Yes, I know you want to be called Carly now..."

Great. The one person to pay attention to my name change was dead and obnoxious. I knew he wanted me to thank him. I didn't.

"I treated you terribly while we were married, but it was to spare you..."

He stopped himself, probably because he couldn't think of a lie to go along with that one. What could he possibly have been sparing me from? Humiliation? Newsflash. Having a husband like him was very humiliating.

"Let's just keep things to the murder case. If you didn't kill the strippers then how did they get in your backyard... *my backyard.*" I corrected myself.

He swooshed over to the lumpy purple accent chair that sat next to the door of our room, the one he always loved but I couldn't stand and apparently couldn't change. "That is a very good question." He paused like he was thinking it over. "Someone must've brought them here to frame me."

My chest tightened. "Listen to yourself. You expect me to believe someone carted dead bodies up Gate Hill to frame you? I guess it has to be that coroner who made up your heart attack... This is pretty delusional, even for you, Jackson."

"I don't know. I'm just trying to help you with your investigation."

"My investigation?"

"The one you promised you'd do for me. Now, I think it's pretty apparent that the investigation should also include clearing my name. The person who framed me is probably the same person who killed me. Probably. I would start with Destiny, and my cousin."

"I'm going back to Indianapolis tomorrow morning, so I'm sorry, I won't be able to help you solve your heart attack. Caleb can have the house, so ask him for help. I draw the line at missing women being found in the yard, especially since we all know nude dancers were your favorite."

"Now, now. I don't play favorites when it comes to nude

women. I love them all, frankly... makes no difference to me whether they're dancers or accountants."

He seemed to know his joke wasn't funny at a time like this. He dropped his smile and went on. "The families of these women deserve to know the truth about what happened, don't you think?"

I hated him for playing on my heart strings. These women deserved justice, at the least. And I did believe him that he hadn't committed the murders.

But that didn't mean I was going to stop Rosalie from coming over here tomorrow morning to get rid of him.

CHAPTER 10

CURSES

*T*hankfully, when the police came with another search warrant to inspect the inside of my house the next day, there really wasn't much to inspect. My stuff was still in boxes and Jackson's personal things had already been removed after his death. Plus, Mrs. Harpton had done a thorough cleaning.

I sat on the couch with Rosalie, next to the box she brought. It had bright yellow crescents painted all over its sides that were probably moons even though my stomach was hoping croissants. Caleb passed us every once in a while to smirk and "apologize for the inconvenience."

"They think Jackson did it, huh?" Rosalie said. "I was hoping that was a rumor."

"I talked to him last night. He says he didn't do it. And he really hasn't got much to gain by lying right now."

She chuckled. "Ghosts lie all the time. They're surprisingly worried about their reputation, if you can believe it. Legacies are one of the few things still important to them." Seeing my face, she added. "I'm sure Jackson's telling the truth, though."

Caleb came back down, carrying my laptop.

"Wait a minute. That's mine," I said.

"I know," he replied.

"Oh dear Lord, they think you're in on it," Rosalie said, and I shushed her.

I ran a hand down my face. I hadn't expected to be dragged into this so deeply. "When will I get that back?"

Caleb left without answering me along with the professionals from Landover.

As soon as the door closed, Rosalie took her box to the dining room table and opened it up. Not croissants. I checked. Just weird trinkets, gems, and bundled twigs.

"This house is just as amazing as I thought," she said, obviously trying to cheer me up. She looked around the dining room. "I bet this is the exact way this house looked back when Jackson's great grandparents owned it. You've got some serious antiques. No wonder Caleb is crazed with jealousy."

I nodded slowly. I wasn't really in the mood to give her a tour, even though I knew she was hinting. I'd just had my privacy violated, my laptop confiscated, and my dead ex-husband accused of murder.

She didn't seem to catch on that now might not be a good time for me. "I sure remember the rumors about this place back when I was a kid," she said. "Something nobody forgets. The curse, especially."

She suddenly had my attention. "What curse? What are you talking about?"

A smile formed across her thick pale cheeks that seemed to say, "All in good time," a look I absolutely despised. My mom used that look a lot whenever I'd ask about my adoption or my biological parents.

"I feel a lot of energy in here," she said, pulling out a hand-held meter device from the box.

I sat down in the chair next to Rosalie. Out of my peripheral vision, I noticed Jackson on my other side.

"Oh good," he said sarcastically. "You've called in Rosalie Cooper, the town fruitcake, to help with my case. They have the police, and we have the corny mystic who paints cardboard boxes."

I looked back at Rosalie. She didn't seem to hear a word the ghost next to us had said. She was going on and on about energy and the little contraption she was holding. "It's called an EMF meter. You've probably seen these on TV in the ghost hunter kind of shows."

Jackson rested his elbows on the table and cupped his chin into his hands like he was pretending to be enthralled. "She's an amazing medium, huh? She knows exactly when there's a ghost afoot. We are witnessing credible science right here."

She set the contraption on the table and Jackson flicked it with a finger. It moved a little.

"Oooooh, did you see that," she said, her voice rising in enthusiasm. "That movement means there's likely a ghost right here in this room, right now."

"You don't say!" Jackson said, gasping, something I didn't know non-breathing entities could do. "Did you hear that, Carly doll? A ghost."

I shot him a look, then went back to Rosalie. She caught on. "Are you experiencing Jackson's ghost right now?"

I pointed. "He's sitting in that chair. He flicked the doohickey."

Rosalie looked over but I could tell she didn't see anything. "I see," she said in that tone people use with the unstable. "You mentioned getting rid of him. Do you still feel that's appropriate?"

I turned to my ex. "With every fiber of my being."

Jackson's face dropped. "This is insulting. I can't believe you're going to try to get rid of me after you promised to help me."

"I promised to help you, and I will. That doesn't mean you need to be around when that happens."

Rosalie pretended to be interested in her box of stuff and the movement of the doohickey, but I could tell she was listening to me, watching me with a curiosity that should have made me feel self-conscious, and normally would have, if I weren't so used to arguing with my ex.

I went on. "You had far too much control over my life when we were married. I'm not sure why I gave you that control, but it's a regret I have to live with. You, on the other hand, are not something I have to live with. So bah-bye."

Rosalie heard her cue and quickly dug into the cardboard box in front of her, pulling out a thick bundle of sticks and a lighter. Jackson disappeared when he saw it, making me think this "fruitcake" might actually be onto something.

Rosalie held the bundle up as she spoke. "This is sage. It's been used to get rid of ghosts for centuries. When it comes to apparitions, you simply have to tell them that you no longer want them in the house. But there can be no ambiguity. You have to forcefully tell them to leave immediately and mean it, wishing them nothing but the best, of course. And then, after you've done that, we perform a smudging, which is just what we call it when we 'cleanse' a house with burning sage to rid it of spirits, and welcome the peace."

"It will get rid of Jackson for good?" I asked, not really caring what in the world it was called or why we were doing it, just so long as we reached the outcome we wanted.

"Yes," she said. "Ghosts build energy the more they're

allowed to stay in a house, meaning the longer you don't ask them to leave, the more power you're giving them to stay."

I swallowed. "Okay, spark up the sage. Let's do this."

Jackson reappeared. "I can't believe you don't find my presence useful, or at least entertaining."

I ignored him, again.

He continued. "Shouldn't you take her on a tour and ask about the curse some more before you get rid of me? I might be able to confirm a few things for you?"

The man was desperate, so at least I knew this sage-thing was probably going to work later if I needed it.

"Oh, all right. You're stalling, old man, but all right," I said.

Rosalie was looking at me sideways. I could tell she was starting to question my sanity about as much as I was.

"Jackson thinks we should go on a quick tour before we begin exorcising his ghost, or whatever this is. He said he'll try to confirm the rumors you've heard about the house."

She tossed the sage bundle onto the table and stood up. Her 60-year-old face practically glowed with excitement in the little bits of light streaming through the curtains. "Sometimes, even a jerk has a great idea."

Rosalie swayed awkwardly when she walked like one side of her had to propel the other side forward. But she'd always refused to go to the doctor, the stubborn woman. She stopped every once in a while on the stairs to catch her breath. "When I was a kid, we always heard Gate House had a curse on it. It was built by Jackson's great grandfather, Henry Bowman, a man who made his money exploiting women." She raised her eyebrows at me, apparently expecting me to catch on. I didn't.

"He owned a number of," she lowered her voice. "Houses of ill-repute, back in his day, before he got married and had children. It was how he made his millions."

"Millions? Off a brothel?"

"Several. He had a whole chain in New York," she said, matter-of-factly. She held onto the railing tightly, and the perfectly smooth decorative wood swayed under her weight. "This was back before there was birth control, or proper meds for STDs, so many women went mad from syphilis. Many were forced to have abortions and even more had children. Unwanted children. I heard Henry Bowman put those children to work as soon as they could sit up..."

I gasped.

"Not like that. He had them make awful clothing for the women, do the cleaning and stuff. Finding dresses for his high-end call girls wasn't exactly something you could just head over to the mall and pick off the racks. This was back in the late 1800s, back when women wore heavy dark dresses that reached the floor and went all the way up to their necks..."

I thought of Mrs. Harpton.

"We heard he treated all of his workers terribly, long hours, kids with stunted growth from malnutrition, fingers worked to the bone, poor things." She shook her head. "But, one time, he took in the wrong girl..."

We headed down the hall toward the nursery, our footsteps creaking along the floorboards underneath us. I looked around for Jackson, wondering why he wasn't confirming or denying things. That was his job here.

"How do you know all of this, and I don't?" I asked.

"It's just the rumor. You know how small town's are. Probably nothing."

"That's exactly what you said about Jackson being connected to the missing strippers."

She looked down at her feet as we stopped in front of a large door down the hall to our right that was decorated around its trim with birds gripping leaves. Rosalie grabbed the knob and opened it. It was just a wall.

"There are two of those like that here," I said. "If you figure out why, let me know."

She turned to the room on our left and opened the door there.

"Oh good. An actual room," she said when it creaked open to more than just drywall.

"Only the nursery," I said, trying to get the woman to move on. I quickly pointed down the hall. "The maid's quarters are on this level too, the real bedrooms are one more flight up."

"One more flight up, huh?" she said, sighing like she might not make it.

The darkened hall around the nursery felt about five degrees colder than the rest of the house. And I always got the feeling the old Victorian didn't want me on this floor. So I rarely even paused on my way up, instead pretending this whole floor didn't exist. Rosalie, apparently, didn't share that feeling. She motioned for me to follow her into the pale pink, mostly empty nursery.

The room smelled like a well oiled antique and was spacious for a nursery, with two twin beds pushed up against the back wall next to a tiny wooden crib with the kind of solid, boxed-in sides that seemed more like a cage than a bed for human babies. A large fireplace took up most the wall by the door, its opening a gigantic mouth ready to swallow any small child dumb enough to sleep here. And above the mantle hung one of the creepiest things of all: a strange wooden horse art piece with large, bugged-out, dead eyes and a tongue flopping loosely to the side.

Still, as creepy as all of that was, none of it bothered me as much as the thing in the armoire.

I tried to distract Rosalie and get us out of the nursery before she could notice it. "You should see the maid's quarters," I said, taking a step for the door. "If you think this room is bad..."

She lifted her little doohickey contraption above her head and over to the fireplace. It went crazy with movement, and Jackson wasn't even flicking it this time. "This house holds more than one ghost. You know that, right?" She could barely talk, her voice heavy and out of breath. I wondered if it was nerves or the stairs.

"Never thought about it," I replied, pointing toward the door. "I can only communicate with Jackson, though. Should we see the rest of the house? And weren't you going to finish talking about the curse? Who was the wrong girl that Henry Bowman took in?"

"Yes, yes," she said. I could tell she was more interested in the room and her spinning-out-of-control EMF meter than finishing her story. "The woman who put the curse on the family. This is all rumor, dear, just some kids talking. And this town has had some crazy rumors."

I chuckled. "Like the Dead Forest being a home to shapeshifters?"

She looked at me sideways. "Yes, that's one of the craziest."

The white armoire off by the fireplace suddenly caught the woman's attention and she waddled over to it, throwing open the cabinet door as if drawn to do so. She let out a small guttural scream under her breath when she saw what was there front and center. The reason Jackson always called me Carly doll. The thing I hated the most.

A doll mostly stuffed sat on the first shelf next to an old worn-out Bible. It had an overly large porcelain head, hands, and feet. Gently, Rosalie picked it up and studied it a moment.

"What the..." She lifted the thing up to my face, her gaze shooting from the doll to me and back again; the thing's lumpy little legs dangled and clanked together by my ear. Its hair was painted on but it was light brown with curls just like mine and its face... the resemblance was spooky, especially with how well the delicate paint job had held up over the years. From the shape and color of her hazel eyes to the mole on her neck, we were the same.

She had a black dress, very similar in material to the high-necked one Mrs. Harpton always wore, only hers was a lot shorter.

"I know," I said. "Isn't it creepy? Jackson always called me Carly doll because I look just like that thing. Her name's Eliza, I guess. I actually pity the little girl who played with such an odd, creepy doll long enough to have named it."

Rosalie didn't say a word. She gently set the doll back down and backed away from the cabinet. "Like I said before, I honestly think we should do a seance, here in this house, and soon," she finally said after about a half a minute of silence.

"What about the smudging thing and asking Jackson to leave?"

I went to shut the cabinet. The creepy doll stared at me with eyes that looked exactly the same as my own, almost pleading with me not to close the cupboard door and leave it. I turned away and headed out to the safety of the cold, dark hall, quicker than I'd intended.

Rosalie stumbled behind me. "I could be wrong," she said. "But I'm pretty sure the woman I was talking about, the wrong one Henry took in because she cursed his family forever, was named Eliza, too."

CHAPTER 11

MY DESTINY AWAITS

*R*osalie and I decided to do the seance next Wednesday night. But she left me the sage and some do-it-yourself instructions on the smudging in case I wanted to get rid of Jackson myself. She strongly encouraged me not to, though. "If this house is cursed," she said, tugging on one of her long dreadlocks. "Jackson might just be your liaison to it."

I stared at her a second like that made sense. As soon as she left, I stuffed the sage into the top drawer of the credenza, catching a glimpse of what had to be one of the last photos taken of my dead ex-husband. The police had rummaged through everything, and what was tucked at the bottom of some drawers was now at the top, and vice versa.

I pulled the photo out and examined it. It was strange to see Jackson in full color and non-transparent. His beard was grayer than I remembered it being when I left four years ago, his hair just as dark. He was standing with his cousins and his uncle at what was apparently his uncle's re-election campaign kick-off party or something just a few months back. Caleb's father was mayor of Potter Grove. Balloons and mayoral posters plastered the background of the photo.

I shouldn't miss the old days.

"I'm even more handsome in person, wouldn't you say?" he said behind me.

I quickly stuffed the photo back in the drawer. "I will use that sage someday. You know that right? This... whatever this is, it isn't normal." I wanted to ask him about the doll upstairs and the rumors about the curse, but he disappeared again, and I didn't feel his presence.

One thing was for sure, I was going to do as much research as I could on Gate House before Rosalie and I did our seance next week. I also wanted to pay a visit to Destiny to find out about the last few years of Jackson's life. He said someone had been trying to kill him. Maybe she knew more about that. .

I knew she wasn't going to be happy to see me. I was right.

DESTINY LIKED the early shift at the Starlight Lounge. I'd heard her regulars were older men who needed to fit their jollies in sometime between dinner at 5:00 and being tucked into their Depends at 9:00. After a quick call to make sure she was there the next day, I was on my way. The police had already finished up at my house, and thankfully, I hadn't had to talk to the press yet.

I stopped by the Shop-Quik and picked up a bottle of Destiny's favorite rum. I only knew this because it was in one of the first boxes the movers brought to Gate House the day I moved out four years ago. I held the bottle for a full minute, talking myself out of spitting in it.

Right now, standing in the liquor aisle of the Shop-Quik, all I could think about was Tina and how her schizophrenia had first manifested itself at this very shop years ago. I needed to call her to see how she was doing and be the friend I regretted not being. "Tomorrow," I told myself like always.

Once again, I talked myself out of spitting in the bottle. Instead, I tossed it into the trunk of my Civic, along with a two-liter of Pepsi and a couple of plastic cups I took from the fountain drink area when no one was looking.

The Starlight was in Landover, a city that got its name because so many people referred to it as that "Land over there." It was the big city near us, and a lot of people in Potter Grove commuted in for work, school, or, apparently, watching strippers.

I parked in the lot under the large sign that read, "Totally Nude Dancers," and shook my head. I couldn't believe I was actually doing this. This place represented the beginning of the end for my marriage to Jackson. It was all part of the humiliation that kept me from reconnecting with this town for the last four years, and yet here I was, about to go through those carefully blacked-out memories to save my perverted husband's reputation.

What in the hell was I thinking?

I strutted over to the door and yanked it open before I could talk myself out of it. A humungous man with neck tattoos and an intimidating glare sat on a little stool just inside. "Ten dollar cover," he said.

"I just want to talk to one of the dancers."

"Doesn't matter. Same for everyone."

I only had ten dollars in my purse. And I was planning on using that as a "tip" to get Destiny to talk to me if I couldn't leave a message with management that there was booze in my car waiting for her.

The club was much classier than the neon sign out front led me to believe it'd be. But then, I'd only seen strip clubs in movies so I imagined nothing but sparkly gold curtains holding back all sorts of weird splatter in the back. The room I was looking at was a nice cocktail lounge area, tastefully decorated with crisp white linens on the few tables it held and napkins stuffed in glasses in the shape of fans.

These ladies were making bigger bucks than I could afford, even in a small city like Landover, Wisconsin. Destiny wasn't going to be enticed by the lukewarm booze sitting in my trunk or my ten-dollar bill. She probably had Dom Perignon chilling in a VIP room somewhere, about to cuddle up to another rich old guy with a drinking problem and a wad of cash bigger than any other wad he had on him.

"Can I leave a message with you then?" I asked the bouncer.

"Nope." He took his phone out from his back pocket and clicked open an app like I was no longer standing there.

"I'm an old friend of Destiny Bowman's," I lied. "I just want to leave a message for her. Can you please tell her..."

He turned away like the conversation was done.

I yanked my wallet out of my purse and fished out my last ten dollars, gripping it tightly like it hurt to let go of it for something so stupid and unnecessary.

He snatched the money. "Tell her yourself," he said, pointing to the door that I was one-hundred-percent certain led to the splatter part.

I gulped. "Okay," I said. "Can I borrow some paper and a pencil?"

I plopped down at one of the tables, tearing the paper in

half, erasing and rewriting the ridiculous note to Destiny. I waved off the blonde in the halter top again and again when she came around to ask if I was ready to order.

It wasn't perfect, but I'd already used every part of the paper and I was sure neck-tattoo-guy wasn't going to give me another one without charging me.

Hi Destiny. I'd really like to talk about the creepy murderer we were both apparently married to. I have Captain Morgan's and Pepsi waiting for you in my car, so please text me to let me know if you want to talk at your break. I don't think anyone else will understand what we're going through.

I scrawled my name and number at the bottom. Then, held my note out to the bouncer.

"I'm not the messenger," he said, pointing, once again, to that door.

"You could consider the ten dollars payment for helping me with this favor."

He went back to his phone and I took a deep breath. "You're not Carly Mae anymore," I reminded myself as I opened the door. Still, my heart raced and my nervous facial tic spasmed just thinking about the whole slew of women behind this door, ones my disgusting husband used to prefer when we were married, along with a group of men who were just like my disgusting husband.

Thankfully, no one turned and noticed the door opening. I walked right by the back of many patrons' heads. Most were sitting, zombie-like, along the various parts of the stage, but there were also a few at the nicely decorated tables, similar to the lobby. I kept my head down, not wanting to make eye contact with anyone here, only looking up to make sure I was heading toward the right naked lady.

Destiny and I made eye contact and she shot me a dirty look. She was a large woman for a dancer, taller than Jackson, and probably weighing just as much, thick but not fat, with straw-like bleach blonde hair that she liked to keep in little-girl ponytails.

I hugged my arms tightly around my chest and ignored the fact the only other women in the room were flopping and wiggling around poles totally nude. I marched over to Destiny, fully thinking she'd back up and shy away. She didn't. She sashay-danced over to me like I was an expected part of the show. I could feel the other patrons' eyes on me now. They were all staring like I might rip my clothes off and dance with the women on stage. I didn't look at them. I kept my eyes on the naked woman in front of me, just like what was proper under the circumstances.

Somehow I lifted a shaky hand and tossed the mostly crumpled paper at the floor by Destiny's feet. Then, I turned and speed-walked up the aisle, mumbling a few "Sorry's" to the disappointed patrons, instantly kicking myself for caring about disappointing a room full of perverted Jacksons.

I couldn't get to my car fast enough.

～

A LITTLE AFTER 8:00, she finally texted. "I have a break in ten. Have my drink ready."

I did. She came out the back door wearing a bright pink robe and flip flops. Even though she was in her mid-twenties now, she still had the round soft face of a teenager. I could see why men preferred this look. It was almost a cartoon version of what most women looked like. Long fake eyelashes and tons of eyeliner, thick pouty, glossed-up lips. And did this woman even have pores?

She grabbed the plastic cup and took a sip. "Needs ice," she said in a high-pitched, breathy voice.

"Sorry. I honestly forgot that part. Next time." Like we had scads of next-times ahead of us, bonding in the alley of her strip club, drinking from my Civic.

The sun was already setting, and I had to get back to the house soon. "Sorry I threw the paper at you. I tried to get the bouncer to give you the note."

"Jimbo?" She said. "He takes his security job seriously since the... you know."

"Since the murders? He does a good job."

"He's all right. At least he's normal, not like the creepy guy they got workin' the other times." Destiny took a longer sip this time then leaned against the trunk of my car. "So, I saw the news. Jackson was a murderer."

"That's what they're thinking," I said.

"I'm surprised you wanted to meet with me," she said. "But I guess we both got screwed by that guy. I got screwed out of a pretty significant chunk of change, though."

It was a loaded response. The hatred between us seemed to grow thicker the more we pretended it wasn't there. I didn't want to talk about the house or the inheritance, so I tried to move on.

"But," I said. "We're lucky to be alive. Cheers." I held up my cup that really only had Pepsi in it. She hit her plastic one against mine.

"Those last two girls worked here," she said.

"Did you know them?"

She shook her head. "Not really. Jackson and I had a

private dance once with a couple of the girls. But I wasn't working here at the time. I quit dancing when I married Jackson. The liar told me I'd never have to work again. Except, here I am."

"I saw the inside of this club. You make good money. Better than I'm making. The inheritance I got is in a trust until Rex dies."

She laughed into her cup. "Figures."

I told her about how I couldn't change a thing in the house or sell it until the dog passed away, and that I was given a stipend that barely paid for electricity. That seemed to make her smile.

I went on. "I should've known there'd be a screw-you catch involved. My pre-nup was six-inches thick. I'm not sure what made me think the inheritance would be any different."

"Yep, a meeting with Jackson's lawyer is one you'll never benefit from. Ronald, the awful little man with the handle-bar mustache who wants you to hurry up and sign so you won't actually read anything in the contract."

We both laughed, and I was almost caught off guard by how funny and smart she was. I was grilling her for information, but it did feel good to have someone to talk to about Jackson and the oddities of Gate House.

I tried to regain my focus. "Jackson told me he changed his will because he thought someone was trying to kill him. Did he ever mention that to you?"

Her mouth dropped. "What do you mean *Jackson told you?* When did you talk to him?" She held her cup out for me to fill up again.

The smell of booze mixed with old trash filled the air around the backdoor of the strip club. I fumbled with my words and thoughts as I hit the key fob and opened my hatch again. "He wrote a note that was included in the inheritance." Thankfully, I was a pretty fast liar. "The note said something about a poisoning and a hospital."

I grabbed the Captain Morgans and filled her cup up again.

"Just so you know, Jackson was going a little crazy there toward the end, I hate to admit. I hear it runs in some families. I don't know anything about an attempted murder, though." She took another sip, looking up at the pinkish-yellow streaks across the sky. "But I do remember one time I had to pick him up at the hospital after he had too much to drink. It was poisoning, all right. Alcohol poisoning. I'm thinking about writing one of those tell-all books about being married to a delusional, crazy, drunken murderer. Maybe Jackson can help me quit dancing after all."

Damn it. I should've thought of that one first. I was the writer.

"Did he ever tell you someone cut his brakes?"

"This sounds a lot like an interrogation," she said. "I honestly don't remember if he did. Why?" I felt every dagger pointing from her eyes.

"No reason. I still can't believe he might've killed those women. I never saw any signs of instability. I mean, aside from his drinking and womanizing."

"Those are not signs of instability or potential murdering." She motioned toward the club beside us. "Or that whole place would be full of killers. It's actually therapy for a lot of these guys. Wives don't understand them, pressures building," she said, looking at the backdoor. "I've gotta get back."

I poured the rest of my Pepsi out, watching it fall over the tufts of grass poking up from the concrete. Something small scurried behind the building, and I jumped, suddenly very aware I was standing in a dark alley... with a stripper in a robe, pouring drinks from my trunk while a murderer might still be on the loose.

She chugged the last bit of her drink and tossed her cup into the back of my car like it was a traveling dumpster. "Can't say it was nice. But, thanks for the drinks." She walked away then turned back. "Don't contact me anymore. You won. Enjoy your inheritance. And your murder house. Game over."

CHAPTER 12

SO, YOU DID KNOW THOSE STRIPPERS

I couldn't wait to confront Jackson that night, if he had the nerve to 'manifest himself'. He did. I was putting away the dishes (just after 10:00, I'd missed the house agreement again, damn it) when I realized he was next to me, staring at me in the same way he used to back when we were first dating. I thought it was endearing back then, before I knew the difference between endearing and creepy.

"You know," he said, when I spotted him. "I'm not going to age anymore. So we can be together for more than 20 years before you're older than me. And I'll try not to let your age bother me after that, so long as you don't lose your looks too much."

I walked right through him to get to the cabinet with the plates. A rush of cold caught me by surprise, along with the smell of peonies. "What the... did you just bring me flowers?"

"They're your favorite. I bet Brock doesn't know that."

"Who cares."

"Here's another one of your favorites."

I tried not to notice, but I couldn't help it. The smell took over the whole kitchen. "Pancakes," I said, nodding, my stomach growling even though I wasn't hungry and the smell was fake.

"Just how you like them, undercooked and drenched in that sickeningly sweet imitation maple syrup. I never understood why you liked that one, honestly. I also remember you cry during the end of every Harry Potter movie. You say you don't want kids but you have a notebook full of baby names and room ideas..."

"Okay, stop it," I said, holding in a smile. "It's borderline stalky and creepy, and nobody cares." I poured myself a nice large rum and coke with ice, and took it to the living room.

I had the TV on, and the Landover murders were all over the news again today. I could hear the reporter going on and on about the bones discovered in the backyard of the local dead professor's house, and how he apparently had a love for all things lewd. "The remains have not yet been identified as those of Candace Newman and Heather Telamario..."

"I talked to Destiny today," I said as I sat down on the couch. "She had a lot of interesting things to say about you. For one, she thinks you killed those women. She's going to write a book about it."

"Aww, it's charming how she still can't get enough of me. A little stalky and creepy, though." He sat down on the settee, stretching out.

"I asked her about the poisoning incident you're so convinced proves you were murdered. She said it was alcohol poisoning."

"A murderer would say that."

"And she says you two had a private session with the murdered women."

The camera angles focusing on my house made the turrets

look even stranger than usual on the TV screen, more lopsided if that was possible. Scarier.

In contrast, the newscaster's voice took on a pleasant, authoritative tone as the b-footage played. "This locally famous house, known by residents as Gate House for its two security gates and large hill, is believed by many to be cursed. Built in the early 1900s..."

"Once I build up enough energy, I'll show you the night of the alleged alcohol poisoning," Jackson said. "I don't remember much, but I'll be able to walk you through it step by step. You can see for yourself if it was alcohol poisoning. It was also the night you were talking about, the one where Destiny and I met those dancers in the VIP lounge."

"So, you did know those strippers."

"I never said I didn't. You can know them, too, in a channeling."

I had no idea what that meant.

Unfortunately, he elaborated. "You have very strong mediumship. It's why you can see and talk to me while others can't. Another neat trick I'm sure you'll be able to master is channeling."

I pictured those people in seances who convulsed about, allowing spirits to take over their bodies. "Yeah, no thanks," I said. "I've seen a channeling before."

He leaned back into the velvet throw pillows on the settee. They actually depressed a little under his ghostly weight. "Those were parlor tricks, most of them, performed by charlatans. But channeling does involve you allowing me, or another spirit, to control your mind... and body for a while." He raised his eyebrows up at me when he said that last part, and I just about puked. There was no way that was happening, ever.

He continued. "When mastered, channeling is amazingly accurate, and I'm sure quite fun, like you're right there actually experiencing things just the way they were when they happened for that ghost. Moment by moment. Breath by breath. I can't remember things accurately, but I can take you to a specific memory when we combine our energy through channeling. And it will be one-hundred percent accurate in real time."

"Sounds interesting. Still passing. No offense, but I can't allow you, or any other spirit for that matter, to have control over my mind and body for even an iota of a second."

He pointed toward the TV of a photo of the youngest stripper, Candace, being shown alongside the footage of police officers packing up the remains lifted from our yard. "She was Destiny's favorite at the strip club."

I coughed on my rum and coke. "She said she barely knew the girls."

"Destiny quit dancing when we got married, but we still liked to frequent the clubs together, an arousing excursion to take with your spouse..."

"I'll take your word for it," I said.

"Anyway, Destiny seemed particularly interested in this girl right here. Candace. Invited her back to the champagne room with us a couple times. And like I said before, one of those nights was the night I was poisoned."

"You're doing that on purpose," I said.

"What?"

"Making me want to know more about that night so a channeling will sound like a good idea."

He shrugged. "I've never done a channeling before, obviously. I've only been dead a few months now, but I think I can build up enough energy for it."

I turned to him. He was a darkened figure sitting on the settee, his transparency fading into the crimson fabric the more we talked. "So how do you know how all of this ghost-stuff works, anyway? Are you handed some sort of handbook or something?"

"It's more like a knowledge..." he searched for the right word. "Lump."

I stared at him.

"Yes. Lump. Just like a lump of knowledge is made clear to you as soon as you realize you're dead, and you suddenly know everything is going to be okay. Nothing in life matters anymore."

"Then why are you so concerned with who killed you, if you were really murdered?"

"I was murdered," he said. "And death is not a one-size-fits-all process. Even though some of us logically know nothing matters anymore, it's a bit harder to disconnect from the living than you would think."

"It's hard to move on, just like Rosalie said." I sat back and crossed my arms. I had a million questions, and I still had that bundle of sage in case I decided Jackson needed to move on quicker than he was ready for. "You said you needed to build enough energy to do a channeling. Just out of curiosity, how long will it take you to do that?"

His eyes widened and a slow smile formed across his dark bearded mouth. "I thought you'd never ask."

CHAPTER 13

CHICKENS AND EGGS

I invited Brock over for brunch the next morning, a daring move that Carly Mae would never have made, but I was just Carly now, a different person. And Just-Carly no longer lived in her mother's basement, listening to the woman lecture about the biology of shriveling eggs that would never be babies. Just-Carly knew life was life and it would happen the way it was meant to happen. Nothing mattered in the end anyway, apparently.

I spent all of Saturday morning cleaning the house and trying to memorize the house agreement. Rex followed my every move, jumping up on my skinny jeans excitedly whenever I put the dishes away correctly, making me wonder if he really did care about this silly agreement. He was a dog. How could he even know?

I was just making sure the Tupperware was organized by size, according to the diagram provided in the house agreement, when the phone rang. I threw down a plastic lid and answered it.

She didn't even let me say *hello.* "I saw the news. That was your house, wasn't it? I recognized it straight away, plus your horrible ex-husband was all but formally named the murderer."

My mother. I should've called her. I'd spent so much time avoiding thoughts of her I didn't think to call her when it mattered.

Her voice was fast, almost southern sounding, a part of her childhood that spontaneously popped up when she was anxious. She continued, "I'm just glad you're alive. Who knew you were living with a murderer for eight years of your life? And to think, the only thing I used to worry about was why on earth you weren't having children. Now, I have to say, I'm glad you didn't. We'd have little half-murderers running around right now. Don't get me wrong. That isn't to say, you shouldn't be worried about time. You don't want to wait too long to start thinking about children like I did."

Even when dead bodies are being lifted from my yard, the woman will still finds a way to take a swing at my aging fertility, in the same breath. "Yes, I'm fine," I said, even though she hadn't asked. I told her about the press and the police, about how they took my laptop.

There was a silence that spoke volumes. Why hadn't I called her sooner? I was terrible when it came to guilt-ridden phone calls. It wasn't just the ones to Tina.

"I wonder why they didn't interview you," she said after a minute. "I only ask because I told everyone you'd be on the news, but I never saw you."

I ignored her. "I'm sorry you bragged for nothing. I've actually been avoiding the press."

Someone knocked on the kitchen door. I knew exactly who it was even though I hadn't heard his truck.

"I gotta go, Mom. I've got a friend coming over for brunch."

"A friend? You have friends now? You make brunch? Is it a boy... friend?"

My mother always treated me like the pathetic girl in high school who spent every Friday night reading Agatha Christie with the family cat, not that that's a bad way to spend a Friday night, by the way.

"I'll call you later," I whined into the phone, clicking off before she could say something embarrassing that *my friend* might hear. I reminded myself I was Just-Carly now. I didn't need to be influenced by the past, or my mother who still wanted me to be Basement-Carly-Mae. I pulled open the back door.

Brock leaned casually against the door frame, almost posing, taking up most of it. He looked good in a pair of jeans and a gray t-shirt, his hair still moppy.

"It smells delicious," he said, looking around, teasing me because I told him I'd cook.

"It will." I motioned for him to have a seat at one of the kitchen stools along the back side of the island. "And you're just in time to help. I'm making my famous pancakes from a box." I held up the instant-pancake box already sitting on the island.

I didn't mention the part where I was just making pancakes so I could bring up how they were my favorite, and also how I liked Harry Potter, peonies, and babies. I rethought talking about that last part.

He was good in the kitchen as we mixed pancake mix together and threw the microwavable bacon I'd bought in to the microwave. His arms were massive, bulging, tree-like limbs barely contained in the thin fabric of his t-shirt. I could hardly concentrate on my pancakes. I definitely saw why my ex-husband was jealous. This man was drop-dead gorgeous and my ex was just drop-dead. I wondered what our kids would look like then smacked myself out of it. We hadn't even kissed yet.

Why did my mother have to call? Now all I could think about were babies.

The microwave beeped. "They sure shrivel up," he said, and I almost thought he was talking about my eggs. He pulled a plate out of the microwave with five tiny pieces of what looked like dark brown rubber.

"They definitely don't look as good as what's on your package," I said. "The package." *Ohmygod, Carly, stop talking about packages. And stop thinking about shriveled eggs.*

A gentle breeze blew through the veranda as we sat out on the porch to eat. I almost couldn't go out there. It was the first day the police hadn't been there or the press. And it made me realize how much I had when compared to the women who were found here, how lucky I'd been in life.

"These pancakes are undercooked," Brock said when the top half of the one on his fork broke off from the bottom. "I love that."

I smiled into the air, hoping Jackson was catching all of this. Score one for Team Gorgeous over here.

But I knew Jackson was resting, and I wouldn't be seeing him again for at least a week while he built up his ghostly energy so we could do a channeling together. I could choose to channel in on any chunk of time I wanted. March 30th, the day he was murdered or the 18th, the day of the VIP stripper lounge party with Candace, which was the day of his poisoning. He would take me anywhere. The thought was intriguing, being in someone else's shoes for a moment in time, experiencing things as they saw them, tasted them, felt them. But it required a lot of energy from the spirit doing it so he needed to rest for it.

A small part of me was going to miss him this week. But I also wanted to run research on every living suspect in his murder, if he was murdered, to see if there really was a link there to the women. And I didn't want Jackson asking me about it every two minutes.

"My aunt told me she's coming for a seance next week."

I nodded, my mouth full of pancake.

"You don't really believe in any of that stuff, right? Ghosts and seances. Like dead people can talk. My aunt is crazy." He chuckled, his blue eyes gleaming in the sunlight. "People hovering over their dead bodies or something. Oooooooh." He made a mocking ghost noise.

"I guess we'll see. I'm going to keep an open mind about it, though. Your aunt was getting all sorts of readings on her doohickey thing she brought over. She thinks the house is full of ghosts."

"And what do you think?"

"Well, I don't know," I began. "But I do know that was strange when the kitchen island felt like it bumped into us that first night and then that cookbook fell off the shelf."

He looked off at the woods around us. The cicadas were getting louder, or maybe they just seemed that way whenever there were pauses in conversations.

"I think you've got an old house, and things are bound to fall or shift. There's always a rational explanation for everything." He stared at me a moment like he wanted me to reassure him that the world was still round and that the sun would rise again tomorrow.

I nodded, stuffing my mouth with another humungous

bite. He leaned in and wiped syrup from the side of my face lightly with his pinkie, tracing his finger down over the bow of my lips. His skin felt calloused and wonderful and I never swallowed a large bite of pancake quicker, almost choking when it slid down my throat in a weird clumpy lump. But I knew what was coming, or I hoped I knew. I unclenched my hands from their nervous little balls and told myself to relax.

"I've always liked you, Carly Mae," he said, tilting his head, moving his face in closer. He pressed his mouth over mine and we kissed long and hard while the cicadas sang out their approval and the smell of shriveled bacon mixed with his cologne. I unclenched my fists again and took in every second of the moment.

And I didn't even bother correcting him on my name.

IT WAS EVENING when he left, and as soon as I sat down to watch the news, Rex snuggled into the crook of my arm. The results were back about the bones in the yard. The remains were those of the missing ladies in Landover, exactly what everyone thought.

"We can't say with any amount of certainty, but it has every indication this is a fairly open-and-shut case," Sheriff Bowman said with a suppressed smirk during his press conference, which was apparently recorded earlier. "Of course, we're still investigating every angle, but the ex-owner of the house where the remains were found, deceased professor Jackson Bowman, was known to frequent the nude dancing clubs these ladies worked at." He looked down at the notecards in his hand. "We also have witnesses who say he was seen with both victims not long before their disappearance, so we know he was familiar with these two ladies, and the dancing place they worked at. Plus, the murders and disappearances all ended when Jackson Bowman had his heart attack."

Rex seemed to nuzzle in closer to me, as if he knew it wasn't looking good for our dead friend.

"The cases are identical. The coroner made the determination that these women died in the same manner that the first two ladies did, from strangulation."

The camera panned over to the coroner, standing off to the side of the podium, a plump, short woman with a graying ponytail and apple cheeks. The name "Julie Terris" had been typed on the screen underneath her.

And I suddenly understood what Jackson meant when he said the coroner might have been in on his death. I was pretty sure she was Caleb's sister. I rushed over to the credenza at the back of the dining room and riffled through the top drawer to try to find that family photo from the campaign kick-off.

It was at the bottom behind some old pieces of junk mail and flyers. I pulled it out. That was her, all right. The thick woman with an almost witch-like grin. The caption printed on the bottom of the photo:

Let's Kick-Off Another Great Election!
Mayor Clyde Bowman, Re-Election Campaign Kick-Off Dinner
March 18th

On the TV, Caleb was taking questions now. "No, we are not comfortable in assuming the threat is over. Our department is committed to keeping this community safe, so we will continue to check every possible lead until we determine

Potter Grove and Landover are out of harm's way. But we also feel it is not a coincidence that these terrible acts against women ended when my cousin's life did. Next question."

It sounded an awful lot like the Potter Grove Police Department was pretty much done with their investigation, which was funny because mine was just beginning.

The day of the campaign kick-off, March eighteenth, had also been the day of Jackson's poisoning.

CHAPTER 14

THE CLEAN LIFE

*T*he next morning, I got up early and put on my Sunday-decents, black capris and a flouncy top, perfect for church. I was suddenly feeling the need for fellowship with my community.

And the church everyone went to (if you weren't Catholic or Jewish) was Potter Grove Methodist, a typical brown rectangular building with stained-glass windows and a pointy steeple. Music streamed from the sanctuary when I walked up. I recognized the greeters standing outside right away, mostly because there weren't too many people in Potter Grove I didn't recognize. But these two also happened to be two of the people I was hoping to see that morning. Their faces dropped when they recognized me. I don't think they were hoping to see me as much. Mayor Bowman and his wife. Caleb and Julie's parents.

"Carly Mae. Good to see you." The man lied, handing me a program when I approached him. He cupped my hand with both of his, shaking it extra long just like the politician he was. He looked about 80, which was probably spot-on for his age, thicker than most the other Bowmans, with a dark brown suit that barely fit his middle right. He adjusted his round glasses, and the smell of stale cigar came from every angle as he moved. "How are you enjoying the house?" His voice had that shaky tone older people sometimes got, but it was still as boisterous and confident as ever.

"It's fabulous," I said. "You would have loved it. It comes with a maid and a stipend." Their faces dropped farther. "I feel so blessed to have such an amazing Victorian, built by such an artisan. A true masterpiece that I will pass down to my children, if I have any. If I don't, I guess I'll just... give it to the homeless."

Mrs. Bowman pressed her lips together with so much force I expected her to spit out some teeth. She motioned toward the sanctuary. "Well, enjoy the service," she said. "Good to have you back."

I wasn't leaving that easily.

"You both should come over for tea sometime so you can fill me in on all the old stories about Gate House..."

I wasn't sure if I should mention the rumors about Henry Bowman and his brothels. I decided now was probably not a good time.

"We're moving to freeze the assets," the mayor said, abruptly.

"Clyde, not now," his wife interrupted, grabbing his arm. "It's not official yet."

"She has a right to know," he said to his wife. "It's fairly obvious Jackson wasn't in his right mind when he changed his will, and the families of the victims should be given some money from his estate if he was the murderer. It's only the right thing to do."

"And you always do the right thing," I said.

He tried to hide his smirk. "Some people are saying you're involved. But I don't get into all of that gossip. Covering it up for Jackson. Who knows? You sure seem to love your house a lot."

"We're all sad it came to this," his wife dutifully added, nodding appropriately.

"Yes. That's why I felt I should tell you," the mayor chimed in.

"And, I feel I should tell you something too," I began. "I'm doing my own investigation into Jackson's death. He kept a diary..." I slowed my breathing down, trying to keep it steady as I spewed out my practiced lie, but my face twitched a little. "He said he felt he'd been poisoned about a week before his death. March 18th. The exact day you had him over for your re-election campaign kick-off. Do you remember?"

"I do remember the dinner. The poisoning part, I have no idea what you're talking about. The food was bad, but not that bad." He laughed at his politician joke. "Now, I know you think this is fun and games. But you'd better watch yourself. A lot of people would consider what you're saying to be libel."

"I wonder," I kept going. "If a police report was filed for that day, or if any samples were taken of the dinner. Jackson said he talked to Caleb while he was in the hospital. I also wonder if Julie noticed any poison in his system when she conducted the autopsy. She probably checked, seeing how he claimed to have been poisoned a week before his death. Any good coroner would have checked for that, I'm sure. I'll be asking to see that report and I'm going to talk to a lawyer. I've heard some people say that's a good idea."

Two could play at the "some people" nonsense politicians loved to throw out so they could distance themselves from their own words.

"Sounds like our lawyers will get in touch," he said.

"I hope they do because if Jackson's autopsy wasn't performed to the satisfaction of the estate, we'll have that body exhumed so we can check for poison. I'd better do it quickly while I still have plenty of money." I let my voice emphasize the word "plenty." They didn't need to know I could barely keep the lights on.

The 80-year-old's face turned a dark reddish purple now, the very same color as Mrs. Bowman's pursed lips.

"Do you honestly think," he said through gritted teeth. "The good people of this town are going to be happy about having the body of a murderer dug up just so you can see if he was poisoned?"

"Happy?" The music stopped and I headed inside the church. "I'm not sure what gave the good people of this town the impression I cared whether or not they were happy with me, or my dead ex-husband."

INSIDE THE CHURCH, I quickly found the rest of the family. They always sat up front, first pew, hymn books out and bookmarked to the listed pages. Julie and her husband were there next to their two teenage boys.

"Excuse me," I said to the family behind them, squeezing into their pew so I could sit right behind the blondish gray ponytail I knew belonged to Julie Terris.

They were already in the middle of the "greet your neighbor" part of the service. Julie's face made an unnatural grimace when she turned around to greet me. She was dressed like she'd just run an Amish marathon, long blue denim skirt and tennis shoes. She nodded to me, even though we weren't friends, and never pretended to be.

"I'm still praying for you," she said when she saw me. "God's will be done."

The way she said it made me wonder what kind of will she was praying for.

"It must've been hard to do an autopsy on your cousin," I said. "Especially a man you always hated and were jealous of. The one who got everything from the Bowman estate. You probably thought your side of the family was finally going to get something when Jackson died, seeing how he didn't have any kids."

She studied my face a second, like she was trying to instill the fear of God into me. It didn't work. "Autopsy? Did you say autopsy?" she finally said, her witch eyes softening. "Autopsies are only done if something's suspicious. I always told you Jackson had a lot of demons. A walking Sodom and Gomorrah, if you ask me. Adultery, casual sex, alcoholism, indecency. They are usually defeated with fire and brimstone. And heart attacks."

"Speaking of Sodom and Gomorrah." I leaned in closely, suddenly getting the urge to stir the pot a little more. "You would not believe the stories I heard about the house your family desperately wants. It was built on the backs of prostitutes."

She bit her lip so hard I thought it might bleed.

"Brothels, as in plural. Old Henry Bowman owned a chain of them, I hear. And the children of the prostitutes who worked there, he put them to work too. I'm actually surprised y'all want that house at all."

She turned her attention back to the pulpit even though the pastor hadn't returned yet.

"Houses can't sin," she mumbled.

Caleb came in with his parents, helping them scoot into the open seats next to Julie while the meet-and-greet was still going on. He turned and reached across the people sitting next to me in order to shake my hand. "Good to finally see you here, Carly Mae," he said, as if I didn't know what he was really saying. He knew just how hard it was going to be in this town to prove anything, even if Jackson was innocent and he and his family were guilty. Guilt, innocence, truth, morality. It didn't matter. These were all connected by the blurred lines of whoever was writing the history. And in this case, it was the Bowmans. They controlled every inch of this town.

"When am I getting my laptop back," I asked.

"The Lord giveth and the Lord taketh away," he added, to me before turning back around. The "meet and greet" music stopped and Julie handed him his hymnbook.

I leaned across the knees and purses in my aisle. "Please let him know he'd better giveth back my laptop soon," I replied in his ear. "Or you will heareth from my lawyer."

As soon as I got home, I was going to do as much research as I could, on my crummy phone, about the mayor and his family in the only place at Gate House Brock said the internet connection would be the strongest. Up in that weird turret.

CHAPTER 15

UNSTABLE

I pulled the dog treats down from the cupboard and shook the box. The house agreement said Rex was allowed to have up to three a day, perfect amount for a bribe. He came running just like I'd hoped.

"Good boy," I said, handing him a treat. He gobbled it from my palm, licking my hand, snuggling into it.

"You get one here and two more up in the library," I said, raising my voice up a little at the end like I was selling it, or like he understood. He shook his head "no" and walked away. He had understood. The coward.

My spine tingled and my heart raced just thinking about going up in that turret.

Before I could change my mind, I flung open the small cabinet in the pantry and grabbed the key to the tower from off a nail. There were several keys on nails in that cabinet: ones to each of the three turrets, one to the basement, one to the library, a mysterious one I had no idea what it unlocked. I grabbed the library one too, then headed out the kitchen door.

The veranda circled most of the way around the house and I checked in every direction around me as I made my way over to the turret's entrance at the back of the deck. I was the only one in Potter Grove who still suspected there was a murderer on the loose, but that wasn't the reason I was jumpy.

This creepy house was at its creepiest up in the turret.

I checked over my shoulder for the fifth time, reassuring myself nothing was actually behind me.

The lock was old and so was the key. I knew either one could break off at any moment as I struggled to get them to work together. The door shot from my hand like a gust of wind had sent it flying as soon as the lock was turned. And I was instantly greeted by the musty smell of closed-up, hot, dusty death. Mrs. Harpton obviously didn't clean this part of the house as much as the others. I couldn't blame her. I would refuse to do it too. *I don't do windows or death traps.*

Somehow I got my feet to move forward into the death trap. The bottom floor of the tower was just a sitting area with a ton of old black-and-white framed photos and vintage paintings of Jackson's family propped along the walls like a gallery. I patted myself on the back for that one when I passed them on my way over to the winding staircase. I was the reason they were no longer in the main house. Now I felt like they resented me for it.

Jackson always knew the creepy family photos were the things I despised most about Gate House. So when we got married, he finally agreed to move them all to the lower level of the turret. It took years for this to be implemented. But I'd done it. And I guess Destiny hadn't undone it because most the photos were still here.

All the gilded oval frames with what looked like dead

babies wearing billowy white Christening gowns -- banished to the turret.

The extra-large paintings of women in black lace shawls with scornful eyes that followed you -- see ya later.

All the children with short school uniforms and lifeless expressions standing in front of gardens -- good-bye, creepy-patch kids.

They all had to go, moved to the tower. I'd suggested the basement, but Jackson scoffed at such a thought. His family heirlooms were not going to be hidden away in storage. I didn't care. Hidden away was hidden away.

My footsteps echoed on the hollow planks and off the stone walls as I made my way to the second level of the turret. This was the part that seemed to sway a little in large gusts of wind.

"This tower has stood for more than one-hundred years," the logical part of me reminded myself when I felt it swaying under my feet. "It's past due to fall then," the other part replied back.

I peeked in on the room at this level even though every brain cell I had said not to. It was by far the creepiest room in the creepiest house, so I felt it was my duty to give it one last quick peek to make sure my opinion hadn't changed about it. It hadn't.

A taxidermist's dream. Stuffed birds of all different families behind glass cabinets and display cases, and a few stuffed bears in the corners for good measure.

I had no idea who would put this room together and I didn't care. I kept moving on to the top level, the library. This level had a locked door. I'd heard it was Henry Bowman's secret room. The room where all his master plans were hatched, no doubt, like where to add another strange turret or stuffed bird.

I fumbled with the key to open it, fully expecting to see a stuffed Henry Bowman sitting behind the desk, but thankfully, didn't.

It was a circular room of wall-to-ceiling books with a large mahogany desk sitting squarely in the middle, fountain pen still off to one corner probably exactly where the old man had left it back in 19-whatever. A moveable ladder was attached to the bookcases and if I stood on my toes, I could see the trap door at the ceiling that led out to the balcony at the top of the turret, where Henry would look for cars coming up his hill, no doubt.

There were also stained glass windows at normal height, but they were just for decoration. The sunrise scenes in the various stained-glass colors gave the turret a church-like quality that didn't sit right with me, probably because money from a brothel paid for them.

I gently placed my phone on the center of the desk (because I still didn't have my laptop) and sat down in the old man's chair. Jackson told me, generally speaking, women were not allowed in this library way back when, not without an escort and a good reason, probably written and signed by at least five men.

I put my feet up and leaned back, then took them back down again. I was pretty sure Rosalie was right when she said there were more than one ghost in this house and I didn't need to piss them all off at once. On top of the desk in a frame, instead of a photo, was a yellowed article about Gate House that was dated March 22, 1900.

Mr. Henry Bowman of New York; his wife, Margaret, and their four children are in the process of building what has been described as the most magnificent Victorian house in all of Potter Grove, the newly establishing township just north of Landover. Mr. Bowman, a prominent businessman from New York, New York told the builders to "Spare no expense. This will be a house of luxury that will stand the test of time in beauty and durability. It will establish Potter Grove as a thriving metropolis."

I took a picture of the article with my phone including the grainy photo that accompanied it. Henry, Margaret, their three daughters and their baby son stood in front of the Victorian, blurry workers in the background.

A businessman? I giggled to myself, thinking about how easy it must have been back then to reinvent yourself. No internet to keep track of you. No easy way for information to travel from one state to the next. You could make your millions off the backs of prostitutes and young children and still be called a "prominent businessman" in a newspaper if you told people that's what you were.

I started by looking up poisons that could mimic a heart attack. There were more than I thought. Pretty much any poison could cause the heart to fail, making the death seem natural, but there were even a few that wouldn't show up if I paid to have Jackson's body exhumed. I jotted some down into the notes app of my phone to look up at the library later. Then, I googled the Bowman names, starting with the oldest living relative. Mayor Clyde Bowman.

I clicked on his re-election webpage and almost gagged looking at the promotional pictures of him and his wife, standing in front of the church along with Caleb (in full police uniform), Julie, and the two grandkids. There were other pictures of him shaking hands with Mayor Wittle, the mayor of Landover. According to Jackson, those two had been friends since they were kids, growing up on Landover Lake.

I clicked on his re-election promises. Education. Infrastructure. Nepotism. That last one wasn't official, but it was obvious. His daughter was the medical examiner. His son was the chief of police. Probably every worker and every contract on this website involved friends or family members. And they say all the good ole boys networks were gone. It was pretty blatant, but no one seemed to care. The mayor was lining everyone's pockets, including his own.

One article jumped out at me during my google searches, when I combined both Caleb's and Julie's names. Another dead woman had been found in Potter Grove, four years ago, right around the time I moved away. Strange how nobody talked about her.

Dumped Body Identified
as Missing Prostitute

The mutilated body discovered on the side of the road in Potter Grove on July 14 has been identified as 24-year-old Jasmine Truopp, a prostitute from Chicago, Illinois. Truopp's boyfriend, a known drug offender and gang member, reported her missing two weeks earlier in Chicago.

Police believe she was murdered in another location and dumped in the bushes near the Shop-Quik just off the highway.

"Likely someone in a hurry to get north saw his chance to get rid of the body and make an escape," Sheriff Bowman said.

When asked about the mutilation of the body, which was found naked and in pieces, Coroner Julie Terris attributed it to post-mortem wounds sustained by an animal. "The cause of death was likely strangulation, but further tests are needed," Terris said.

Further tests are needed. Julie was very thorough for everyone other than her cousin, I noticed.

But were these cases related? This one happened four years ago, and its only similarity to the others was the fact Jasmine Truopp had been a possibly strangled woman.

I shook it off. The FBI, the police, or whoever was in charge of finding out who killed these women had probably already looked to see if the cases were related. I tried to find more articles about Jasmine, but nothing turned up. Maybe Mrs. Nebitt could help me out there.

The turret swayed a little in the wind, causing a creaking noise to rise up along the ceiling above me. I stood up and grabbed my phone, checking various desk drawers before I left. All locked. Sometime soon, I would come back to Henry Bowman's library, and I would bring that mysterious key with me.

CHAPTER 16

CONTACT

*B*asically, the only good thing to happen to me those next few days was Brock. We were spending a lot of time together, and since Jackson was resting his energy, I didn't even have to feel guilty about it. Except I did. I knew I should find out from Mrs. Carmichael where Tina was staying. I needed to talk to my old best friend, tell her I was seeing her ex. But every time I picked up the phone to call the Spoony River Cafe, I clicked the phone off again.

I somehow justified everything by deciding I wasn't going to make my relationship with Brock official until I'd told Tina about it. No Facebook announcements. Nothing.

And I knew I'd get my chance that Wednesday. Rosalie said she invited Mrs. Carmichael and Shelby to the seance.

"I'm pretty sure I could've sold tickets," she said, as she set a box of stuff onto the dining room table that Wednesday night. This one was a cardboard box with black moons painted on it. "Everybody wants to come here. The murder house. You are the talk of a very talkative town."

She said this like it was a good thing.

I pulled a black table cloth and some long white candles from the box while I told her about the Bowmans and how they were moving to freeze my ghost's assets. I didn't even know what that meant. "Mrs. Bowman kept saying it wasn't official, so maybe they have to wait until Jackson's actually been declared the murderer. Still, I'm thinking about trying to contact Jackson's lawyer," I said, but I could tell by her face she wasn't sure that was going to help or even be possible.

She pulled her crystal ball out and examined it. "Everybody wants to make contact with the strippers."

"I thought you could only make contact with dead relatives and things. Do you think we could actually contact the murdered women?" Goosebumps shot along my arm thinking about it, mostly because I was worried the women might tell me my ex-husband did them in.

She shrugged. "Spirits sometimes hang around the place they died. Either that, or someplace they have connections to, people or things. They also could just show up. You never know with spirits. I wrote down the names of the ladies so we could call out to them." She pulled a pink post-it note from her pocket with the four names of the deceased women scribbled on it.

Names. That's what we were all reduced to after we died. A name etched into a headstone, written on the back of a photo, or posted on a bright pink sticky note. It seemed like there should be more. I remembered what Jackson had said about death. Nothing mattered anymore. Was that a good thing or a bad thing?

I helped Rosalie spread the cloth over the dark wood of my dining room table smoothing out the wrinkles before we set her crystal ball on top of it. "I could sure use some help at the Purple Pony if you're interested. Part time, of course."

I wasn't sure if she was feeling sorry for me or if she wanted to capitalize on my new-found fame as the owner of the murder house while I was still the talk of the town. It didn't matter either way. "Done. Just let me know when to start."

"And don't worry," she whispered, craning her neck toward the back door like someone might overhear her. "I didn't tell anyone anything about you being able to talk to ghosts, or that you hang out all day with your ex-husband, the ghost and murderer."

"Alleged, on that last part," I found myself saying. I wasn't convinced at all yet.

Shelby's pink Cadillac pulled into the driveway. I could tell because the bumping base of rap music suddenly interrupted the cricket sounds of the night. I could also hear Mrs. Carmichael's voice over the top of it, yelling for Shelby to turn that racket down.

Rosalie practically hissed under her breath before the others came in. "We're gonna try to conjure up the doll lady about the curse too, find out who she was. Eliza."

I was just about to ask her what she knew about the woman when I heard Shelby and Mrs. Carmichael on the veranda.

"No. I'm done. I told ya I'm driving next time," Mrs. Carmichael said, practically coughing up a lung onto my porch. "I don't like any music that loud, but especially not that rap music. For cryin' out loud, you know that."

Shelby patted her pregnancy. "You're just mad 'cause I wouldn't let you smoke."

"I wouldn't smoke around a baby, but he's gonna pop out deaf. You know that, right? That's what you should be worried about."

I was already at the door, opening it for them. They hugged me "hello," and came in, staring all around like they were in a museum. I hadn't expected Shelby's fiancee, Bobby Franklin, to make his way onto my porch too. He grunted his greeting to me, barely even nodding, staggering in like he was drunk. Bobby was a large man with thick curly dark hair and caterpillar eyebrows, like a muppet on the wrong side of the law.

"We brought Bobby for protection," Mrs. Carmichael said, winking.

"It was either this or watch the kids," he mumbled. I backed away from the smell of alcohol coming off the man. I was glad for the kids that he chose this.

"Oh don't listen to him," Shelby said. She batted her spider-like eyelashes at her drunk. "He's been going to every single seance Rosalie's thrown lately. He's more into this than any of us, especially when I mentioned we were having the seance at your house."

I always got the impression Bobby never liked me, and I was still getting that same impression tonight. It was no secret he hated rich people. It was also no secret he drank, but when you combined the two, you were in for a night of complaining about how rich people were ruining his life. Funny how he always considered me "rich," even though it was only ever Jackson.

He scowled when he walked by, giving me a once over before he moved on to my dining room where Rosalie was waiting for everyone. "You and Jackson sure had an easy life. You live up here all by yourself now? Like high falutin royalty, huh?"

If royalty were sitting ducks on a creepy hill, sure.

Dusk was just turning to the dark shades of night. And

judging by the fact Mrs. Carmichael and Shelby were both still in their Spoony River pink uniforms, they probably drove straight here.

Shelby swung a basket full of cute little make-up containers as she looked around my house. "Just some samples for later. A little blush and lipstick I know everyone's just gonna love. Y'all look good in pink, right?"

"I've always been told my seance color's red," Bobby joked, making Shelby laugh a little too hard.

"I haven't been to your house since I helped you move four years ago," she said. Shelby told me at the time she knew I'd return to Potter Grove, but I don't think either one of us ever dreamed I'd return as the owner of this house.

"I'd forgotten how straight-out-of-a-horror-movie it is," she said.

Bobby sat down on one of the dining room chairs. "Yeah, nobody would ever hear you scream way out here in the middle of nowhere. You should be careful."

I knew Bobby was joking, just trying to get under my skin. But he was also creeping me out.

Mrs. Carmichael unpinned her 50's hat and scratched her blonde hair into a bushy mess. "Okay. Let's get this started already. I told Tina I'd visit her early tomorrow. Her roommate's bothering her again," she said, looking around, probably expecting sympathetic nods or people to ask how Tina was doing.

Nobody did, so she went on. "Yeah, her roommate's one of those hypochondriac Mooreheads so, of course, that means she thinks she's dying. I told them to move her. This is a halfway house not hospice. I mean, I feel for the girl, don't get me wrong, but she's always got to have the doctors in there for something that she doesn't have like heart murmurs or mineral deficiencies. You name it, that girl has it. I think it sets Tina off. It's disturbing. It's what's been setting her off lately; I know it."

We nodded, but no one knew what to say. I didn't.

"I can't stay long either," Shelby finally said, breaking the tension. "I got my mom watchin' the kids, and she's not so good with little ones yet. She's only had nine years to get used to grandchildren."

"In her defense, you do have a whole gang of rowdy boys," Mrs. Carmichael said.

"And another one on the way," Shelby said, proudly.

Bobby grunted. "We gonna conjure up some strippers or what?" he asked. He leaned back and scratched at his belly. His tight t-shirt rose up with each scratch, showing the world he had thick dark hair all over. "I hope I didn't come up here for nothin'."

Rosalie lit the candles and smoothed her sticky note onto the table cloth. "Just so everyone knows, I don't have any control over who shows up tonight. We will communicate with the spirits who want to communicate with us." She motioned for me to turn off the lights.

I always knew Gate House was creepy, but I never felt it as much as I did at that moment. It was almost like a dark heaviness surrounded me, sitting on my chest, making me know it was there. I tried to breathe.

"Let's all hold hands," Rosalie said.

CHAPTER 17

THE SEANCE

*S*eances are believed to have originated in the Victorian era right alongside the rise of spiritualism and ghost sightings, or at least that's what I found in the ten-minute research I'd done online before people came over.

A medium would lead a group in making connections to the dead, but it was all done as a fun kind of game, mostly for entertainment to scare yourself silly. Tables lifted, mediums levitated, and sometimes, if you were lucky, a medium would literally spit out something called ectoplasm, a weird gauze-like substance that came straight from her mouth, or other orifice. (Wikipedia did not specify what other orifices those might have been.) Of course, the purpose of the ectoplasm was for the spirits to drape over their nonphysical bodies so they could interact in our physical world.

This was my first seance, and I seriously hoped it wasn't going to be anything like my research.

The only light in the house was the little bits flickering off the candles on the table as Rosalie said a short prayer, asking for guidance in leading the seance. The weird shadows that danced along her face made her look dead herself.

I tried not to pay attention to the heavy feeling sitting on my chest. The more I noticed it the worse it got.

"I see the number four," Rosalie finally announced to the group after about half a minute of silence. "I sense four, all right. Four, four, four."

"The four dead women from Landover," Shelby guessed.

"Yeah, let's hear from those strippers." Bobby sat up.

I wasn't sure why, and I really wanted to tell them to only talk to Rosalie, but the voices came to me, too. Or at me. I could hear them from all over the room, shooting out in various octaves. More than 10 or 20 voices, maybe even 100, overlapping in chatter, shouting in the kind of lilt that lowered and rose at strange intervals. I tried to concentrate on just one. *Four people at the table, not five. She needs to leave. Leave. Leave. Now. Now. Four. Four. Four. Hurry.*

"They want only four people at the table," I said, pretty confident I'd heard them right.

Rosalie nodded. "Carly Mae's right. They're reminding me we can have four or six, but not five. Five is a number that might bring us trouble."

I'd read about that in my brief research about seances too. It was considered a bad number, one that would bring up evil spirits, not sure why. Like the ectoplasm and the orifices, there didn't seem to be much explanation there.

"I'll go," Rosalie said, standing up from the table. The heaviness in my chest eased up when she said this. I couldn't help but feel something was rewarding me for interpreting things correctly. I took a deep breath while I could.

"What? Are you crazy?" I asked in between my breaths. "You're leading this thing. I'll go." The heaviness against my rib cage seemed to squeeze again, like an extra heavy lead apron they use for x-rays.

Rosalie handed me her pink sticky note before she scooted her chair back and walked away from the table. "I get the feeling they want you to lead this."

Mrs. Carmichael sucked in a gasp that got her smoker's cough going again.

"Don't worry," Rosalie said. "You're all in good hands with Carly Mae."

Bobby grunted. "I knew we came all the way up here for nothing."

I had no idea how to lead a seance. But, I went along with it, seeing how my new employer at the Purple Pony asked me to do it, and the weird heavy feeling had demanded it. I said a little prayer first, just like Rosalie, except mine went something like this, "Please God don't let me spit out any ectoplasm, from anywhere."

I looked at the pink note, and slowly read a name. And even though no one told me to, I found myself instinctively trying to make my voice spooky. "Candace Newman, are you here? Heather Telamario." I took a moment to try to feel the heaviness again. Nothing. "We welcome you here."

Apparently, absent today. After a beat or two, I tried the other names. "Trish Jenkins. Kelly Moore... Jasmine Truopp."

"Jasmine Truopp?" Shelby asked. "Who's that?"

I was just about to hand the seance back over to the real medium, when just like before, lots of voices came out at once. Many spirits all around.

No one here by that. Stop searching. Names no longer matter. You... you matter. You must save us.

I realized my head was tilted, as if I was listening intently to something I didn't quite understand. I tried not to let it show, but Shelby picked up on it. "What? Did you hear something? What did they say?"

"Nothing," I said, practically shushing her. I had no idea what the voices were talking about.

I continued. "Are the dancers here? The ones whose bones were found in this yard? Candace? Heather? Are you here?" I asked again.

No. No. No. No.

"Who is here? Who are you?"

It doesn't matter. You are here. The sweet, sweet living is all that matters now. The living will help the cursed. But the living must be careful. The living must tread lightly. You will figure out how to help us...

Other voices chimed in, higher pitched ones. Children-sounding this time.

Please. Help us. Help us. We are trapped here. The curse. You're the only one who can save us...

It felt like I was on a roller coaster, not in the moving sense but in the adrenalin rush one. I felt dizzy, drained, and ramped up all at the same time. My heart raced and my palms felt sweaty and warm. "It's okay," I said to the voices around me, even though I had no idea if it actually was. "I will try to help you." These were children. Scared children, and I wanted to hold them, protect them, but I had no idea how. The closest I ever came to children was a notebook full of names. "I'm very confused," I finally admitted to the scared voices.

Realizing the seance group thought I was talking to them, I focused my attention back to the table. "I've never even been to a seance. There are lots of voices, talking about some sort of a curse. They're telling me to tread lightly. They're trapped here. They're screaming for help. A lot of them sound like children."

Mrs. Carmichael smacked her hand on the table. "The Bowman curse is real. I knew it. This old house is haunted, all right. Haunted by all the women and children the Bowman family worked to the bone in their brothels."

Bobby mumbled. "No wonder the old professor liked his hookers. Runs in the family, eh?"

Shelby practically screamed from her seat. "What curse? What are y'all talking about?"

"Eliza?" I said, ignoring the fuss. I could feel them all leaving and I knew I needed to act fast. "Are you here? Eliza."

Rosalie's doohickey flickered crazily on the table. I felt fear more than anything, not my own, even though I was pretty afraid. Something cold passed through me, along with an almost unrecognizably soft whisper, right up next to my left ear. "Do not tell anyone I am here. Do not contact me by name again." The candles blew out, and the doohickey stopped flickering.

I shook my head. "I... I think the spirits left." Although my mouth formed the words, I didn't believe it. I knew some of them were still here, just not talking anymore, or not able to.

Rosalie turned on the lights and everyone blinked wildly, trying to breathe normally again. Inhale, exhale... we were almost in unison, smiling oddly at one another.

"Did you feel that?" Mrs. Carmichael said, rubbing her arm. "Goosebumps. I have honest-to-goodness goosebumps." She put her hand on Shelby's arm.

"That was creepy," Shelby said.

Bobby shook his head. "You mean crappy. I thought we were gonna connect with some dead strippers. Or, my dead Nana could've floated by to reveal her secret bratwurst recipe."

All I could do was sit motionless for a second. I'd just

gotten off the roller-coaster and a part of me knew I needed to calm down and process things. The other part wanted to get right back in line and do it again. That last message had to be Eliza. We had a connection, a shared secret of sorts.

"What in the world was that all about?" Shelby asked, patting her belly. "The baby started kicking like crazy when you asked for that last person, Eliza, like he wanted to kick his way out. Who is Eliza? Or Jasmine? And y'all have to tell me everything you know about this curse."

Rosalie limped back over to the table. "It's believed the Bowman family was cursed way back when this house was first built, and Eliza is the woman said to have put that curse on them. But no one knows who she was."

"Oh-kay," Shelby said like she thought we were all crazy. "Who's Jasmine then?"

"She was the woman found in the bushes outside the Shop-Quik four years ago," I said. "I thought there might've been a connection between her death and the others."

Mrs. Carmichael scratched at her head, making her hair even puffier. "I remember that vividly. They found her a few days before Tina had her first episode." Her voice was low and croaky. I knew it was hard for Mrs. Carmichael to talk about that. It was hard for me to hear it, too. She went on. "I panicked at first. You can't get an official call from the police department in the middle of the night that doesn't make you panic. I tell ya that much for sure. I thought Caleb was sayin' they'd found Tina's body, same as that girl. I was crying too hard to hear him. But thank God she was still alive."

I put my hand on Mrs. Carmichael's shoulder. It was the perfect time for me to ask for Tina's address or phone number. Somehow I couldn't get myself to.

"Not bad for a first seance," Rosalie finally said, breaking the awkward silence that had come over the group.

"You're kidding, right?" Bobby groaned. "I cannot believe we drove all the way up here for that."

"I'll try to throw up some ectoplasm for you next time." I dead panned.

He raised an eyebrow at me. "Is that an exorcist thing? At least that would've been entertaining."

Shelby shook her head at her fiancé, trying to get him to shut up, but he didn't notice. He went on. "We were supposed to hear from your dead husband about how he strangled strippers, buried them in your yard. Or maybe hear from the skanks themselves about what it was like to have a crazy professor pull their fingers off one by one..."

"Okay. That's enough," Shelby said, her face almost turning as pink as her hair.

"You cannot tell me I'm the only one who feels that way."

Shelby smacked his arm. "Yes, that's what I'm saying." She turned to the rest of us. "Don't mind him. He's just mad 'cause they cut his hours again at the Starlight." Shelby got up and grabbed her basket full of samples.

"I didn't know you worked at the Starlight," I said to Bobby.

Shelby handed me a lipstick and motioned for me to try it on. "I told him he needed to get a real job because we were gonna have a real baby soon," Shelby replied, kissing Bobby's thick cheek. "And he did. He's one of the best bouncers ever."

"It's not easy putting up with those people all day. The lowest of the low," he said, like he was expecting us to agree with his sainthood.

"Pretty soon," Shelby went on, "he's gonna be able to buy a

new truck. Well, not a new-new truck, but new to him, and he's gonna contribute to the rent —"

Rosalie chimed in. "What happened to his old truck?"

"He crashed it four months ago coming home from work."

"Stop making a big deal out of it, Shelby. And stop treating me like I'm four. So, I looked down at the wrong time," he said. "Won't happen again."

"No. It can't. It better not. Not with a baby in the truck," Mrs. Carmichael said. "I'm glad you're doing good now, though."

Shelby and Bobby exchanged strained looks while the rest of us pretended not to notice.

Rosalie put her hand on my shoulder. "Did I tell ya, Carly Mae's gonna work at the Purple Pony? You can start tomorrow at noon if you want."

Shelby squealed. "I'll give you a stack of my business cards." She looked over at Mrs. Carmichael. "Just in case any tourists need makeup. Come on, now. You know those old Landover ladies have money."

Rosalie brought out her tarot cards and told Bobby he could go first, which seemed to make his tightened face relax into a half smile. But all I could hear was Destiny's voice talking about the creepy other bouncer who didn't seem normal at the Starlight. Bobby must've been the guy she was talking about, a man a little too angry with strippers.

CHAPTER 18

THE FREAK SHOW

$\mathcal{M}$rs. Nebitt unlocked the doors right at 9:30.

"Morning," I said. She didn't smile or respond, but she didn't shush me either. Progress.

She waddled back behind the incredibly high counter that separated us and climbed onto her stool without really looking at me. It was, after all, a Thursday again. I briefly thought about telling her I had a job now at the Purple Pony, but I knew she wouldn't be impressed. Her eyes were glued to her computer. I went over to the periodicals section.

After searching through Gazette after Gazette for anything on Jasmine Truopp and Tina's "episode" that happened around the same time, I gave up. I needed the older stuff. The good stuff.

The stuff that required help.

I stared at the little old lady sitting behind the counter and tried to will her attention to me.

She never looked up.

I approached her desk, and leaned into her. "Can you help me do some research?"

She scrunched her nose like she'd just smelled a burning septic tank. "Depends on what kind of research you're doing?"

She turned her head suspiciously to the side like I might ask for help finding the "Chronically Unemployed's Guide to Cooking Meth" or something to that effect. What I had to ask would be equally as horrifying in her eyes. "I would like as much information as possible about a woman murdered here four years ago. A prostitute."

She looked at the ceiling a second, and I tried not to care what the horrible old woman thought of me. I knew she was wondering if this was a colleague of mine or a friend. She thought of me as a prostitute too. I was just about to go back to the Gazettes when she scooted her stool forward.

"I think I know who you're talking about. She was from Chicago, actually, or so they thought." She tapped on her computer and turned the screen toward me. "Jasmine Truopp?"

"That's her."

"I'll bring the articles up on the microfilm machine," she said, quickly making her way over to the large file cabinets against the far wall of the periodicals section. She seemed to have a swing in her step as she moved. Maybe she wasn't awful after all. Maybe she was just bored.

She finished setting up the machine for me. "Always ask for help with this. Got it?" she said. Mrs. Nebitt was one of those people who needed things done her way. Don't open the microfilm drawers without help. Don't try to put books back on the shelf yourself. Things must go in their exact spots and ordinary people are incapable of doing complicated things like alphabetizing.

I thanked the librarian then, before she turned away, I whispered. "You were right about Jackson all along."

She stared at me a second, her eyes the size of dinner plates under her coke bottles. "I don't know what you're talking about," she finally said, cracking a smile as she waddled away.

The Gazette was a weekly newspaper, so Tina's article was in the same edition as Jasmine's remains. I read Jasmine's article first. It really didn't offer anything new except that the body had been found naked by a resident who didn't want to be identified, which was strange. Most people in this town lived for publicity, no matter the reason.

It was only when I read Tina's article that my hunch the two might have been related really came to be a real possibility. The article was dated a few days later. Tina had tried "to take the store over," whatever that meant, saying she had weapons of mass destruction.

"She was hollering something fierce," Mr. Joe Yelman, the owner of the Shop-Quik, said. "Something about grizzly bears and a naked princess. Of course, I called her mom right away."

Ms. Carmichael is in police custody, currently undergoing psychiatric evaluation.

I stared at the article, knowing how the evaluation went for my friend, knowing that she'd spent the last four years being evaluated, refusing meds, having episodes.

The articles themselves seemed a little too connected to be a coincidence. A naked princess. The Shop-Quik. Maybe Tina had been the resident who found the woman. That could've set her off. Or maybe I just wanted there to be a reason for Tina's break with reality. Sometimes, mental illness just happens. I knew that. It was just hard to accept when you desperately want there to be a reason why you can't go back to the way things used to be.

Sitting in the library's parking lot, I somehow got myself to call the Spoony River and ask for Mrs. Carmichael. She was more than thrilled to give me Tina's address and phone number, making me feel extra guilty for not asking for it sooner. "Tina is gonna love to hear from you. Love it. Love it. Love it. You are so sweet."

I let her believe that was the reason. I was just sweet ole Carly Mae. I didn't tell her I was about to drop a double bomb on my old, now-unstable friend. Not only was I stealing Brock from her, but I was also hoping she could kindly relive that horrible night for me, the one that marked the beginning of her psychosis and ultimately ended in her and Brock breaking up in the first place.

I punched the address into my GPS and sat there a minute staring at it, listening to the automated voice telling me to head south out of the parking lot. Tina wasn't very far away. Freemont, just a 20-minute drive without traffic. If I left in the next half an hour, I would easily make it there and back before work.

My phone rang. It was my mother. My finger hovered over the "ignore" button. I could always talk to her later. But then, she'd been so worried about me lately.

THERE WERE five customers browsing around the Purple Pony when I got there at noon, which was actually good for a Thursday. Even though everyone in town liked to joke about it, Potter Grove really did have a tourist season, but it consisted mostly of a handful of rich people meandering into "that quaint town next door" when they got too bored hanging out at their summer lake houses in Landover. Still, we gossiped about them.

Rosalie waved the one-minute sign to me from behind the cash register to let me know she was finishing up with a customer. The woman looked over at me, and her jaw dropped. She stared for a full ten seconds before finally saying, "You're Carly Mae Bowman, huh?"

"I told you she worked here," Rosalie said, motioning toward me like she was proudly displaying her freak show.

"Taylor," I corrected the woman. "I'm Carly Taylor."

"But you used to be a Bowman. I saw your photo on the news. You were married to Jackson Bowman, right?"

"I was. But I was never a Bowman. I didn't take his last name."

"How cute."

"Yes," I said, biting back my annoyance. "Feminism's adorable."

I was no longer sure I could do this job since it clearly meant interacting with the ladies from the country club, and their multimillion-dollar attitudes. But then, I might just have been in a particularly bad mood. I'd made the mistake of telling my mother about the new job I was heading to at the Purple Pony. She burst into a tirade of insults, mostly about how much my education had cost her.

"Retail?" she said over and over again, her voice rising into that Southern drawl.

"It's a kind of retail job, yes. You know, the hippie shop..."

"Remind me again. How many degrees do you have?"

"I know. I know. It's temporary."

"When I was your age -- and I paid my own way through

college, missy, thank you very much -- I was already working at Stellaplex."

And on and on it went.

Rosalie shot me a look from behind the cash register. "Carly Mae. This is Suzie. Suzie recently lost her husband..."

"Last year," Suzie said. Suzie was a thick blonde in her early 70's with droopy jowls that seemed to be drowning in the blue-and-white striped scarf tied around her neck. "Isaac was always a huge supporter of your good mayor, especially his idea to build the shortcut to Landover."

"Wait. What shortcut?" I asked. The only shortcut I knew of was never a possibility, the one through Gate Hill.

"It doesn't matter now. Your ex-husband wouldn't even hear the proposal, and now I see why. He had some issues he was trying to conceal on his property."

"Yes, dead women can be such an issue." I was in no mood for snotty people around my mother's age.

Rosalie could barely hold her fake smile, her lip spasmed under its weight. She added a quivered laugh, too, like I'd been joking. "This is Suzie's first summer alone on the lake. I told her about our seances."

Our seances?

"She's very interested in connecting with Isaac, and I told her about your strong mediumship."

"I'm the freak show," I said, holding out my hand. "Nice to meet you." I had my own fake smile now.

"Carly," Rosalie spat through gritted teeth. "There's a box of dresses in the back that needs to go out on the rack by the gem collection. Can you get it?"

"I have a master's degree. I'll see if I can figure it out."

"Take your time."

I felt her glare as I stomped into the back to look for the box. I didn't care. I was beginning to feel less like an employee and more like the main attraction at the retail circus. *Come see the serial killer's ex-wife who lives in the murder house. She puts dresses away for minimum wage.* I bet Destiny was making a killing for the Starlight lounge now, too. *And on the dance floor, a nude woman who had sex with the serial killer and didn't end up in his yard.*

I came back out carrying the box just in time to hear Suzie confirming the time for *our seance* this weekend at her lake house. She never looked at me once on her way out.

"You'll get a third of it, don't worry," Rosalie said as soon as the woman left, like maybe that had been the reason I'd been snippy.

It hadn't been, but it was now. "A third?"

"I've got the set up, the shop, and the client connections. That's gotta be worth a little extra."

"Look P.T. Barnum, you're not getting this dog face for nothing." I tore open the box of light brown faux suede business dresses and shoved them into the hangers that were under the rack by my feet.

"Try to smooth out the wrinkles as you go," Rosalie said. She hobbled over to me, picked up one of the dresses from the box, and ran her hands along the fabric to show me the proper way to hang a dress. And I almost cried.

"Is there something wrong?" she asked.

I tried to calm down. I was blowing it, and I needed this job... just until I finished writing that novel I hadn't started yet. I slid my hands over the fabric to smooth out the wrinkles on the Pocahontas-meets-Wall-Street ensemble in front of me, somehow stopping myself from gripping its fabric into my fists and ripping it apart.

Rosalie put her hand on my shoulder. "You okay?"

I couldn't tell her my mother felt like this job was beneath the tens of thousands of dollars she'd paid for my education, or that maybe I felt that way too. So I told her about the channeling I was about to do with Jackson, and how I was a little worried about my ex-husband taking over my body. I looked around the store to make sure the remaining patrons hadn't heard me. I was already the freak show.

I thought Rosalie was going to reassure me there was absolutely nothing to worry about.

She dropped all three dresses in her hand. "Don't do it."

"What? Why?" I laughed, lowering my voice while I looked over at the women in the swimsuit section nearby.

"Human bodies were meant to be controlled by one entity at a time. I've heard it can cause a lot of problems. If the entity's too strong, you might..."

"Become possessed? By Jackson?"

"Maybe," she said, picking up the dresses from off the floor and putting them on the rack. She didn't even smooth them out.

"Oh wouldn't that be something? That was probably his plan all along," I said.

"Just don't do it. Or maybe do more research on it before you do it. I hear it's much harder on humans than it is on ghosts. You're just learning to use your powers of mediumship. Let's do another seance, with Suzie this time, and see how it goes. Take it slow."

"I want forty percent."

She stood back and examined the dresses. "They're cute, huh?"

I nodded, even though they were far from my style. "Not as cute as under-the-table extra money for a seance."

"Okay, we'll split it sixty-forty."

She looked at the patrons who were meandering around the gem section then lowered her voice. "Let me just say one more thing. If you do start channeling, only channel with entities you trust, Carly Mae, please. And only for short periods. Keep track of how long you do it and how you feel afterwards."

It was already time for the five-o'clock news by the time I got home. I heated up Rex's dog food, grabbed a beer, then went to the living room to relax and watch it.

Local news stations still covered the stripper murders at every broadcast, but from a different angle. It was now mostly the "aren't we all relieved to have this murderer off our streets" one. Destiny had a mic up to her pouty pink lips as she stood outside the Starlight. The title "Destiny Bowman, Alleged Murderer's Widow" was proudly displayed underneath her.

"Tell us what it was like, being married to Jackson Bowman, suspected serial killer," the reporter said with a tone so serious and sure of himself I could tell, to him and probably the rest of the world, the murderer had already been convicted.

"It's surreal," Destiny said. "It's no secret Jackson left his wife for me. I wonder now if I was intended to be his first victim. He had a thing for dancers, obviously. The whole story will be coming out in my tell-all book."

I scowled and took another gulp of my beer, mocking her voice in my head. *It's no secret he left his wife for me...*

"Yes, tell us about your book." The newsman beamed.

"Rumor has it there's already a bidding war going on between two major publishers..."

I coughed on my beer, choking and gagging, and not just because I hated the taste. *I was the one with the murder house, and the degrees in English. First, she stole my husband and now she was stealing my secret dream too?*

My mother was going to be very disappointed I hadn't capitalized on my dead ex-husband first.

"And there you have it," the reporter said, gleefully like the news station had received some sort of an exclusive. "What it's like to be married to a murderer..."

"Whatever happened to innocent until proven guilty?" a voice behind me said. I practically fell off the sofa. I was so happy to hear him. My awful ex-husband who might have murdered the very strippers he liked to cheat on me with.

His voice was clearer tonight, unlike some of the other nights when he sounded like he was talking into a garbage can. And he was almost in perfect color.

"So," he said as if Destiny and the reporter didn't matter anymore. "Are you ready to do a channeling? I feel amazing."

CHAPTER 19

CHARGED UP

I couldn't wait to tell Jackson about my research so far. About how creepy Bobby Franklin had been and how he worked at the Starlight, about how I conjured up Eliza at the seance, about Jasmine Truopp and Tina's possible connection there. He kept nodding in that same pretentious way he did when he practically demanded he help me with my master's thesis.

"Great work covering all angles, but I'm worried it's not enough. Tell me again why you haven't met with Tina yet."

I stood up, mind numb. I stumbled into the kitchen and poured the rest of my beer down the drain. I was seeking his approval again. Just like that stupid school girl with her three-ring notebook full of naiveté. I hadn't changed. He hadn't changed. Nothing had changed in our relationship except the man was no longer breathing. Brock was right. There must've been some sort of weird "daddy issues" here. One thing was sure, I needed to grow up already, take back control, and actually claim my independence. It meant more than a name change.

"Sorry. I can't do the channeling tonight," I said. "I have a date with Brock."

"You drove all the way up the hill to sit around, drink beer, watch the five-o'clock news, and then go back down into town again?"

I nodded.

"Well, cancel your date or whatever. I'm all charged up," he said like I cared about that. "We really should do this when I'm at the peak of charged, don't you think?"

I shrugged. "Then, go charge yourself while I'm gone." I grabbed my cell phone and keys from off the kitchen counter.

As soon as I got down Gate Hill enough for there to be cell phone coverage, I called Brock. "Wanna meet for dinner?"

"Sure," he said. "I'm just finishing up work. I was gonna head to the Bulldog tonight anyway. Meet me in about an hour?"

The Bulldog? That was a sports bar in Landover. Why would he want to go there? Was this some sort of new-girl-friend test or something? I didn't really want to pretend to be interested in whatever stupid game was on tonight.

I drove by the Starlight on my way over to the restaurant, just to see if I'd see anything interesting. I'd be channeling here later on. Maybe. Plus, I had some time to kill before I needed to be at the Bulldog.

There were quite a few cars in the parking lot for a Thursday evening, or maybe it was just more than I expected. I actually had no idea how many people went to these places on any given day.

I didn't see anything unusual, except Shelby Winehouse's Cadillac, which probably meant Bobby was here. I parked and watched the entrance, growing bored after my five-second stakeout didn't produce anything incriminating.

I crouched down in my seat so no one would see me then drove around to the alley like a little old lady who could barely see over her steering wheel. I almost side-swiped the police car in front of me, parked the opposite way just outside the Starlight's back door. It was Justin, sitting in the exact spot I'd been when Destiny and I were guzzling rum and cokes from my car. His eyes bugged out when he saw me. I might've been the last person he expected. He was talking to Bobby.

"Hey Justin. Hey Bobby," I said as I pulled up, trying to make my voice sound normal and relaxed. "What's Potter Grove's finest doing patrolling Landover?"

He stared at me. "This investigation involves both cities."

"Good to see you haven't given up. I saw Caleb on the news saying it was an open-and-shut case."

"She still thinks her husband didn't do it," Bobby laughed, puffing on his cigarette.

"Ex-husband. And no, Bobby. I don't," I answered. "I heard it could've been a creepy bouncer, though."

He shot me a look, and I gulped, surprised I had said that myself.

"What're you doing here?" Justin asked.

I hadn't thought of that one. "Just taking a shortcut through the alley. I'm late for my date with Brock at the Bulldog," I said then drove away. *Just taking a shortcut through this dark alley by the strip club, officer. Nothing suspicious here.* I really should've thought up a better lie than that. I looked in my rearview mirror. Justin was out of his vehicle now, staring down the alley at me. I hadn't realized until that moment how doubly suspicious it must've been for the ex-wife of the alleged killer to stalk the place where her husband found his victims. Especially since *some people were saying she was involved.*

I hightailed it over to the Bulldog and tried to forget about it.

The Dog, as most the locals called it, was a typical sports bar. Women in tiny shorts and brown tank tops with bulldog faces on them handed out wings and beer to the many men watching them more than the screens around them.

We sat down in a booth across from each other. I could tell his eyes were more focused on the screen above my head than on me.

"You like baseball?" he asked.

I nodded. "I don't follow it that much, but it's fun to watch." I was lying through my teeth. Watching baseball was as much fun as picking lint off of carpet, except after you were done, you weren't even rewarded with a lint-free carpet.

A brunette with big boobs, fake eyelashes, and foundation that seemed two shades too dark for her asked for our order. And I kept my eyes on Brock, watching to see how he was going to look at her. Two could play at this "testing the new relationship" game, a game I wasn't even sure we were playing. I would pretend to like baseball but only if he pretended not to notice the gorgeous woman about to serve us beer and wings. He passed the test. He kept his eyes on the menu only.

When the waitress left, he looked at me. "So they think Jackson did it. I still can't believe you came so close to death."

"It's okay," I replied. I wanted to tell him about my investigation, about Jackson's ghost and how I was pretty sure he hadn't done it, but this was all new ground for me and I had no idea what the appropriate time was to bring up what could potentially be seen as crazy to your significant other, especially since I knew one of his last girlfriends had schizophrenia.

"I'm going to see Tina soon. I'm going to tell her about us."

He nodded, looking more at the screen than anywhere else. He caught my eye and seemed to realize he should probably be paying attention to me. "I think that's a great... great... holy smokes, did you see that? I cannot believe he dropped that. Crazy."

"Crazy," I repeated, like I'd just been watching that same thing on the screen above his head. "Do you still visit her?"

"Do what?" He was still half-smiling at the screen. He looked at me, and his face took on the reality of the moment, like he was replaying my words in his head and finally cluing in. "You don't have to do this, Carly. It's hard to see Tina. I know because I used to try. But I haven't been there in at least a year, and I can't feel guilty about it anymore. I know that sounds rough."

I nodded, digging my fingernails into the squishy, slightly sticky table.

He ducked his head down until he caught my eye. "Sometimes, it's better to remember things the way they used to be."

The waitress brought our beer. "Here you go, sir," she said when she put down Brock's, tilting her head to the side so her hair would fall over her breasts.

He mumbled "thanks" while keeping his eyes on mine, which was nice. Back when I was married to Jackson, he would sneak in looks at the women around us and I would have to pretend I hadn't noticed.

Is that kind of a man really trustworthy enough to do a channeling with?

I could hardly concentrate on the rest of the night with Brock, and he was mostly watching the game anyway. All I could think about was the channeling I should be doing right now. The murders I should be figuring out, more for the women than my ex, because I honestly believed his murder was tied to theirs.

Once again, I'd let my anger control my rational thinking.

I decided that as soon as I got home I'd tell Jackson to include the dinner with his uncle into our channeling session. If Mayor Bowman was really trying to make a road through Gate Hill and Jackson was refusing, the good mayor had a good reason to poison his nephew and try to inherit a property he could make millions off of. But were they really the type to murder women just to frame Jackson?

Maybe for a free house and a significant inheritance, they would.

But finding out would mean an awful lot of channeling with an entity I wasn't sure I trusted.

CHAPTER 20

CHANNELS OF TRUST

*I*t was almost midnight when I found myself standing in the middle of my living room with my arms stretched out and my eyes closed, just like Jackson told me to do. He explained that his energy would pass into mine and we'd become one, so to speak. The trick was that I had to keep my mind clear. (Of course when he said that, all I could think about was that Stay Puft Marshmallow scene from *Ghostbusters*.)

I giggled.

He shot me a look. "Your mind's not clear. I can only do this once tonight. Then I'll be too exhausted to go on. In fact, you won't see me for awhile afterwards. I have to recuperate."

That was enough of a reason right there.

I opened my eyes and turned to face him. The lights in the living room were off, a touch Jackson said was necessary because it calmed him, but I could still see his silhouette in the faint light coming from the kitchen. He was a handsome man, not in the Hollywood "rugged bodybuilder" sense like Brock or Justin. He was more like one of those weak, geeky types with the crooked smile that you find yourself drawn to.

He smiled at me, and I realized I was staring at him.

"Rosalie doesn't think this is a good idea," I said.

"I know. You told me. You don't have to do this, Carly. It's entirely up to you. However, you are a very strong medium, and I think you'll be fine."

I sat down on the settee. Too many people were telling me what I did and didn't have to do in life.

"I want to sit for this," I said.

"Whatever you want."

"And I want you to take me to the night of your poisoning," I said. "First, the dinner with your uncle's re-election campaign. Then onto the Starlight and the champagne room."

"I have to warn you," he said. "From what I've heard about channelings, living beings *feel* things exactly as the ghosts felt them, and by that I mean smell, taste, touch..."

I took a deep breath. I wasn't exactly sure I wanted to taste anything from the VIP room at a nude dancing club. "How... uh," I coughed on my words, trying to think of a delicate way to ask. "How much tasting and touching went on that night?"

"Never enough," he said, an answer I should have anticipated from my perverted ex.

"I'm ready," I said, even though I wasn't. I knew I needed to do this quick, though, before I lost my nerve. I lifted my hands out and closed my eyes, thinking of nothing. He grabbed the tips of my fingers, all ten at the same time, and I giggled some more.

"Okay. Okay. I got this," I said. "I'm just nervous."

He didn't answer me. He waited until my breath was calm and my heart rate normal.

I felt him entering me, not in the sexual sense, but in a "whoa, that is weird" one. It started slowly, with feather-light touches that began at the tips of my fingers, traveling through my hands, up my arms, over my belly and then wrapping its way around my chest, something I wondered if it happened during every channeling or just an added movement from my ex. He was a perverted ghost after all.

I held my breath and tried to relax into it. It was like a rush of cold wind that began outside my skin and continued inside.

"Good," he said from inside my head. His voice was inner, like my own voice now, but different. "Do you feel me?"

I nodded, but my head didn't feel like it was moving through air anymore. It felt like I was moving through some sort of plasma, like jello.

The only annoying part was the breathing. Loud and exaggerated, it reminded me of the first and only time I ever went scuba diving on our vacation to Mexico. No training, no regulations. Just *here's a wetsuit, breathe into this apparatus, and good luck.* I ended up freaking out in the first three minutes and had to swim back to shore. Jackson swam back with me, even though I could tell he didn't want to.

"Relax," Jackson said. "We're not in Cabo anymore."

Were we sharing that memory of scuba diving just then?

"Stop thinking about your breathing, and you won't hear it as much. You can open your eyes."

I opened them. It was fuzzy at first, kind of like swimming with goggles. And a pain spread across my abdomen as if someone had punched me in the stomach, an odd, lingering aching.

I realized it was the feeling of full. Jackson took another bite of what tasted like medium-rare, melt-in-your-mouth, bacon-wrapped steak with -- what was that -- yes, mushrooms. And as if at once, I knew I was going to love this channeling thing. And I no longer heard my annoying breathing at all.

Instead, the sounds of clinking glasses and laughter surrounded me. I recognized the hall immediately as being a part of the country club. Nice tables with fine white table cloths and waiters hustling about. An extra-large red, white, and blue banner was pinned above the huge stone fireplace with "Re-Elect Mayor Bowman" sprawled across the face of it. The smells of steak, corn, and potatoes wafted up from plates. Jackson slipped his plastic cup full of coke under the table and added some rum from his pocket.

I hissed under my breath when I noticed. "Please tell me you were not that kind of a drunk in your last days. I'm beginning to believe the heart attack was a real one."

"Trust me. You'd booze it up too if you had to snooze through the family gatherings I had to go to. Listen to this guy."

I turned my attention to the rest of the table where Jackson's uncle and cousins were sitting, along with the mayor from Landover and his wife. Mayor Bowman was in the middle of telling a story, and everyone else was pretending to pay attention, nodding and smiling.

The mayor's voice was loud and confident, like he wanted the other tables to hear his amazing story too. "And that's why Mason had to pawn Grandpa Earl's watch to pay for the damage. But then, that was my brother for you. He would've sold Gate House too, I'm sure of it, if anyone had given him the chance."

Mayor Wittle laughed from his corn. "That is one heck of a

story," he said, this thin turkey neck looked like it might snap under the weight of his lightbulb-shaped head.

Jackson brought his drink back on the table and swished it around noisily with his fork like he didn't care who saw him doing it.

"Don't lecture me," he said to me in his head. "I take a cab to the Starlight."

The mayor pouted sympathetically at my ex. "Sorry. You would've loved that Rolex, Jackson. Passed down for generations," the mayor said to my ex. "But like I was saying, your father was a businessman not a sentimental one."

Jackson pulled his sleeve up to reveal an antique Rolex. "This Rolex? My father tracked the watch down a year after he pawned it. He had to pay double, but he got it back. A bit more sentimental than he's given credit for, I'm afraid. In other words, he would never, ever approve of anyone selling even a smidgen of Gate House property to build a road. So you can stop telling me stories about my father now. You can stop pretending this is about family."

Mrs. Wittle's mouth fell open and I saw corn stuck along her graying teeth.

"Settle down, Jackson," Caleb said from across the table. "Nobody said anything about the road. We know how you feel about it." He turned to Julie and muttered the last part, but loud enough for the table to hear. "Even though, technically, and we all know this, part of that inheritance should've gone to our father when Grandfather died. We should've contested it."

Julie nodded.

"The inheritance is always passed down to one Bowman only," Jackson said, chugging his drink. "I'm sorry, but our grandfather made his choice. And so did my father. I will too, someday."

I watched their faces tighten. "They're about to come after you with their steak knives," I said. "You know that, right?"

"I suppose those steak knives are pointed at you now." He chuckled in my head.

Jackson looked out the window at the lake and the long pier with about 20 boats tied up along the side, thumping against their ropes. He sipped his rum and coke. "We're all like those boats tied up along the pier," he said to the table, pointing until they all turned to look at them. "Only here because we were roped into it."

"Jackass," the mayor said.

Jackson talked back to me in his head again. "Honestly, I didn't care what they thought of me at the time. Looking back, I guess I should have. I was only here because I was obligated to do family things if the press was involved."

He looked over at a squatty blonde with a camera, taking pictures of the various tables, asking people questions with a recorder in her hands.

"So, I gave the required donation. I stayed the appropriate amount of time," he said to me as he downed his last gulps of drink.

"And you got the proper amount of poison," I added.

Jackson went back to eating even though we were full. I could see why. I always ate when I was avoiding conversation too, but I was happy he did. I've never tasted such delicious steak. Maybe food just tasted better in a channeling.

"If you'll excuse me," Mayor Bowman said to the table, standing up. "I have a speech to make."

He whispered something to the waiter who was busy handing out slices of cake before he moved onto the podium.

Out of the corner of my eye, I watched the waiter intensely, noting what cake pieces he gave out. He handed the Wittles theirs from the outer part of his circular tray, then moved onto Julie and her husband, same spots. Caleb next. Then he went to Jackson where he pulled the cake from dead center. Jackson put it back on the tray and took a different piece from the edge. "Thank you. I prefer a bit more frosting."

"Of course," the man said, then hustled off with the tray.

"I had grown suspicious," he said to me.

"More like paranoid."

"Not paranoid enough," he replied. "I ended up dead, remember?"

Mayor Bowman coughed into the mic and introduced himself, thanking everyone for coming, calling out sponsors by name. Wittle Construction, the company owned by Mayor Wittle's sons and grandsons. They stood up and waved. No doubt they stood a lot to lose on this road never being built or approved. Kick-backs, rigged bids, misappropriated funds...

"And, of course, my amazing family," the mayor went on. "My son and sheriff of this fine city, Caleb Bowman. My daughter, Julie, and her husband, Arnold."

He never once mentioned Jackson. I wondered how that made my ex feel. His parents were gone. And these people were his only family left.

Jackson hunched over and snuck out, barely able to dodge the waiters with their cake trays. He bumped into one and mumbled an already-slurred apology that the waiter did not stick around to hear.

"I headed straight over to the Starlight," he told me as we staggered out the large glass doors of the country club without many people noticing. The cool breeze blew hard against his face, his stomach aching in a stretched-beyond-capacity way. I could tell, he was already pretty out of it.

"Destiny told me she had a surprise for me," he went on. "Close your eyes and relax, and I'll fast forward to the good stuff."

I had no idea what he meant by that.

CHAPTER 21

MOUNTING EVIDENCE

here was less fog this time when I opened my eyes and a lot more clarity. A dozen half-naked women stood all around Jackson as he walked along a dimly lit hallway. Destiny was ahead of him, her bleach blonde hair in its trademark pigtails swooshing along her shoulder blades. Her dress was short, bare in the back, and bright blue like her stilettos.

"Whichever one you like, Jackie," she said, touching his chin, causing my heavy breathing to grow heavier. I reminded myself this wasn't happening to me. This was Jackson's memory. She was only seeing Jackson's chin.

She pointed to the redhead who was coming straight for us in the hall. The woman brushed purposely against Jackson as she passed, pressing herself lightly on his chest. The smell of coconut oil took over my senses. "Oh, excuse me, Jackson," she giggled like she hadn't meant to bump into him. "You two headed to the champagne room?"

Destiny nodded, but the redhead moved on, and so did we, toward the back where the VIP rooms apparently were.

Destiny waved to two women coming out of the bathroom. I recognized them immediately. Candace and Heather. It was surreal seeing the two deceased women I'd only known from pictures on the news.

Candace was a petite brunette with hair extensions and long bright pink nails. Heather was the taller one who liked to toss her sandy blonde highlighted curls from shoulder to shoulder as she laughed, over nothing.

"I recommend this one," Destiny said, pointing to Candace. "You remember her, right? We like her."

"Her," I found myself saying. I pointed to Candace. "Yes. The one from my English class. The other one too, if you can swing it."

Destiny winked at me, running a hand up between Jackson's legs, cupping and stroking him gently. "I thought you'd like her. I bet I know someone who's about to get an A this semester."

She laughed as Jackson traced her inner thigh with the tip of his finger. Destiny held up the one-minute sign. "I'll be right back with your request," she said, sashaying off down the hall.

"You can skip over some things," I yelled in my head to Jackson.

Jackson laughed. "You're saying I should fast forward to the really good stuff."

"I'm saying, keep it PG."

"It's like a virtual reality porno, though. Most people would thank me."

I looked around while Destiny was gone. It was really weird being here, and even weirder being here as my creepy ex-husband. Unfortunately, I could only go where the memory took me but I scanned everyone's face as they passed us in the hall. That's when I saw him. Bobby Franklin, Shelby Winehouse's fiancé. I doubted that bouncer needed to be back here. I was going to keep my eye on him, if I could. Bobby kept his head down, probably hoping not to have to say anything to Jackson.

Jackson made eye contact with him as he passed us. "Shelby would make a lot more money working here," Jackson said to him, and I cringed in my channeling. Cringed. *How in the world did my disgusting ex even make it to 50?*

Bobby looked like he wanted to strangle him. A lot of people gave Jackson that look. "She's pregnant, you ass," he said, and I cringed again. Bobby went on, his hand in a fist now. "And if she even talked about working here." He paused to punch his fist into his other hand. "I'd have issues."

A brunette who looked a lot like the girl from the Bulldog with big boobs and way too much makeup walked out of the bathroom and down the hall. Bobby followed her, staring at her butt the whole time. Poor Shelby. Her boyfriend was a creeper who made fist-motions when he talked about her.

I spoke to Jackson in my mind as soon as the creeper left. "What the hell was that?"

"Just making small talk," he replied. "We joke."

"That's not joking. That's trying really hard to get your ass kicked."

When Destiny came back, she was carrying a large green drink. "Your margarita, sir," she said.

"I don't drink margaritas," Jackson replied. "And I brought my own." He patted his jacket pocket where the flask was.

She stroked the hair around his ears. Destiny's face was close to Jackson's, too close. I never noticed how her chin came to a severe point at the bottom before. "The girl in your class is named Candace in case you don't remember. She's 18, says you're the cutest professor at LU, and guessed that margaritas were your favorite drink so she had me order one for you. Blended with salt. I'll tell her you're not interested."

Jackson grabbed the glass, but in his already sloppy state caused cold margarita to spill along his hand. "Tell her she was one-hundred-percent correct about the margarita." He swigged down a large gulp of the drink, wiping the salt with the back of his sleeve. It tasted way too sweet, weird. I immediately wanted to throw up, probably because I was feeling the way Jackson would have felt after drinking a margarita.

Destiny walked off, and I had a hard time tracking her movement.

"I can't tell if you're drunk or drugged," I said.

Jackson didn't say anything, making me think he was already too far gone.

The floor felt slanted, my brain did too. Slanted and numb. Things were spinning a little. "I need to lie down," Jackson managed to say but it took just about every ounce of energy he had to get the words out.

Candace bounced over to him. Her long waves were a dark contrast to her pale Snow-White-like complexion. "I love your class, Professor Bowman," she said.

"Call me Jackson," he replied. His voice was shaky and weird, but I had no idea if I was hearing it wrong or if he was saying it like that.

She continued like I was making sense. "Destiny's like a big sister to me," she said, curling her arm around his. "Of course, sisters share everything."

Up was down and down was up at this point in the game. Her voice came at me in a jumbled mess. I tried to decipher the code. Jackson was definitely having a hard time following, but I was pretty sure I could do it if I concentrated hard enough. He was under the influence, but I was the part of us that wasn't. If I could separate myself from Jackson, maybe I could clearly see the things going on around here.

"Relax," she said, leading me into what was probably the champagne room. I felt Jackson's shoulders soften, his breathing slow down, as if he was relaxing on her command. She gently set his half-empty margarita down on the coffee table then pushed him hard onto the couch that was just about the only other thing in the room besides a mini bar and some pumped-in dance music.

She climbed on top of Jackson as soon as he flopped onto the dark brown cushions. Candace's very thin silky short robe rode up a little as she climbed her way across Jackson's body, making me realize she wasn't wearing anything else. She grabbed his hands and placed them on her breasts, giggling as she did. I refused to let myself think about it, reminding myself I needed to look around the room instead. But first, of course, I compared our boobs. She was like a full cup bigger than my Bs. Hers were probably fake, though.

Candace was obviously a great distraction for my ex-husband, and it was shocking for me to find out just what really went on in the clubs he used to go to.

You're no longer married to him. You don't care.

It was this thought that helped me detach, to help the room stop spinning as much.

"I always liked you, professor," Candace said with large, pouty lips that were a ridiculously shiny red. Her breath smelled like tic tacs, the green kind. I tried to concentrate on the details, one at a time. I found that when I concentrated hard on the details, I no longer felt out of control. It was like the part of Jackson who was laying half out of his mind on the soft leather couch of the VIP room was not the same as me.

The details seemed to ground me to the place and not the person.

Another figure came into the room. At least one. They were kind of blurry, but I was pretty sure the tall blonde blur coming over to me was Heather Telamario.

Candace's mouth hit mine with unexpected force. It was sticky from way too much gloss as her tongue snaked its way through my lips. "Professor," she said. "How would you grade my performance so far?" Both girls laughed.

I turned my vision to the side, hoping to find what Destiny was doing while this fatal distraction was going on. I had a feeling none of what Jackson was experiencing right now was in compliance with the club's official policies, VIP room or not. Or I hoped they at least wiped down the leather couches in between clients.

Through foggy vision, I saw Destiny standing by my margarita glass, tapping on a syringe to the beat of the Beyonce song playing in the background. *First, a laced margarita and now a syringe?* Jackson was right. He'd been given something, maybe poison. Or maybe he was into injecting drugs. I had no idea what my perverted ex-husband had been into.

While Candace and Heather's hands explored Jackson's drugged-out body, Destiny sashayed over to me with the syringe. I could smell her perfume when she sat down on the floor by the couch and grabbed Jackson's arm that seemed to have no resistance left in it. It flopped into her hands.

"Jackson, honey," she said from some faraway place in my mind. She put something in my hand. "Hold this."

Jackson's hand formed around an object. It was thin and long. At first I thought it was the syringe. It was a pen, maybe.

"Sign your name here." She put my hand on the paper. "You

remember how to do that right? Sign Jackson Bowman. Jackson Bow-man," she said, enunciating her syllables.

My hand flopped to the floor like she'd let go of a dumbbell.

"Come on," she said, her voice raising into frustration. She shook me a little.

I tried to see what he was signing, but Jackson's eyes were barely focusing, and could see much better farther away. I tried to shake my head *no*. Nothing happened. No responses from Jackson at all, except maybe a little drool.

"He's too out of it," I heard what was probably Candace say. "We can try it again later."

Destiny smacked my face hard, again and again. "You've gotta be kidding me. Do you know how hard it was to get him here in the first place? I had to promise him a surprise." She lifted my sleeve up, stroking my arm gently along my elbow and up around my biceps. "This. This is your surprise."

"He needs to sign first," a low voice said from the back of he room.

"His eyes are still open," Candace replied. "Maybe he can still do it."

I scanned the room to see if I could find the bottle Destiny had planned to inject me with before Jackson went farther under.

Destiny put the pen back in my hand. The woman was desperate for me to sign this thing, whatever it was. She finally let my arm drop. "You're good for nothing." She smacked me hard across my face once again as she and the other girls laughed. My heart raced. My eyes twitched, trying to stay open.

"Jackson," I yelled in my mind.

Focus, Jackson, focus. We have to find the bottle before you're all the way under.

He did not respond to me.

My gaze went from the margarita glass to the women who were making out on the coffee table right by it, apparently done with Jackson at this point. They groped at each other's hair, at Candace's robe that was barely hanging onto her body. Destiny pulled it the rest of the way off with one swift movement. Voices and movement spun around me in nude-colored blurs of nausea. I thought I saw a strange blur walking around, but I couldn't really tell who it was.

I realized that's where my ex-husband's last-fleeting attentive moments had been directed that night before he lost consciousness. His eyelids felt like little cartoon anvils had been attached to them. Then there, out of the corner of my eye, I caught a glimpse of the bottle when the three women moved their naked grope-session onto the large chair by the door. A little clear bottle sitting on the coffee table. Its label was only half toward me. Desperately, I tried to make out the words written on it.

ehead

um

ide

Suddenly, and without warning, my heart jumped into hyper-speed. My arms jerked uncontrollably by my side, spasming. With my throat quickly tightening, I tried to swallow, or even to remember the feelings and muscles it took to swallow, but I couldn't. My tongue felt about six times its normal size, my mouth grew drier by the second. Somehow, I managed to lean over just enough to throw up on the side of the couch.

"Ohmygod, I think he's dying," a woman's voice screamed from the chair. I couldn't tell who it was.

"Shit. Not yet. Not good."

"We need to call 911."

"Oh yeah, so they can trace this back to us," a third voice said. It was low, same as the other low voice. Familiar too. A man's voice. "I told you not to give him too much."

WHEN I CAME to in my living room I was on the floor by the settee without any recollection of how I got there. It didn't matter. I was exhausted. My heart was still racing and my head felt like it had just been through a four-month binge-drinking session in Vegas, not that I knew what that felt like. I looked around the dark room for my ex-husband, mostly so we could go over what he remembered from that night. He was nowhere to be found. I remembered him saying something about needing to recuperate.

I was pretty sure the margarita had been laced with GHB, a club drug. GHB was why guidance counselors warned young girls not to leave their drinks alone for even a second. It was the stuff frat boys cooked up in their bathtubs so they could take unsuspecting girls behind a dumpster and later claim it was consensual. People on GHB were not only drugged senseless, but they'd also do whatever someone else commanded them to do, and they'd have no recollection of it the next day. Who knew the only time I'd experience GHB firsthand would be through the memory of a 50-something-year-old man?

Destiny gave Jackson the drug so he'd sign something, probably a new will or an amendment to her prenup. Whatever. Destiny needed to explain herself. She was clearly about to commit murder right there.

Had Candace and Heather blackmailed her or gotten in the way somehow? Had she murdered them too?

I sat down on the settee again, letting my head throb into my fingertips. The name on the bottle was still standing on the edge of my mind, like it couldn't decide if it wanted to dive in and commit itself to being a memory or if it wanted to remain a forgotten piece of life. I bolted up, ran over to the credenza in the dining room, and yanked open the top drawer. I pulled out a piece of paper and a pencil and began scribbling down everything while it was still fresh in my mind. The two women. The words on the bottle. The exact feelings I had after being drugged.

Of course, that's when the house started to shake just like it had when Mrs. Harpton was cleaning, only stronger. I looked around for the housekeeper. My third written reprimand was laying on the dining room table beside me.

Dear Ms. Taylor,

As detailed in the house agreement, after three formal reprimands, appropriate actions can be expected. These corrective actions will take place tonight.

Great. This must be the punishment for not following the agreement.

Somehow, I staggered to the kitchen even though the floor was shaking so hard I could barely get one foot to shuffle in front of the other. I leaned over the sink and threw up. Again and again. The shaking, and the nausea, lasted all night.

CHAPTER 22

CLINICALLY EVALUATED

I was really surprised not to have a hangover the next day when Rex woke me up, gently nudging my hand with his nose, reminding me to feed him, already. I'd fallen asleep on the settee somehow. Everything was a blur, and like most things in my life, I had more questions than answers. The channeling still reeled in my mind, but not in the same way it had last night.

Jackson had known he'd been drugged. And he knew who'd done it. Maybe all that drinking at the dinner had morphed into the drugging at the strip club, but what he'd forgotten in his fogged-up memories was pretty clear to me. Destiny was the killer. And the two now-deceased girls she was with were her accomplices.

"Sorry, Rex," I said, grabbing my phone from off the coffee table. "I'll feed you in a minute. I know I'm late." He put his head down, obviously disappointed. This was going down on my permanent record, another corrective action would probably be taking place soon.

I looked up everything I could about GHB before the

internet conked out on me. The more I read, the more I knew that's probably what Jackson had been given the night he thought he'd been poisoned. I also looked up poisons that ended in ehead um ide, the only words I could read on the bottle. The results were weird, especially when I added heart attack to my search. Sodium fluoride came up along with a dart gun the CIA apparently made in the 1970s that would cause victims to have heart attacks. I bookmarked that one for a click-bait article if I ever went back to the dark side of writing again. Then, I came across an interesting article about potassium chloride, one of the injections they give death-row inmates when they euthanize them. Apparently, it was too painful to be given alone. The person would have to be given a knock-out drug first -- GHB! It made sense if there was also an ehead involved, which there wasn't.

I took Rex's bowl from the microwave and set it down for him. The kitchen clock said 10:18. Shoot. I'd have to leave for the Purple Pony soon. No part of me wanted to go, but I couldn't call in sick on my second day.

I dragged myself over to bathroom and splashed water all along my face, fully expecting to see Jackson behind me. I was dying to go over all the details of our channeling session, along with my new suspicions, but he wasn't there and wouldn't be for a while.

On my way out, I noticed I had a message on the answering machine. I hated using that archaic devise, mostly because I never remembered to check it, so my messages were usually super old. But because coverage on my cell phone up here was pretty much nonexistent, I had to deal with it.

It was Brock. "Hey you," he said, making me smile at the warmth in his voice. "I talked to Justin, and, anyway, I'm sorry I took you to the Bulldog last night. Let's plan something more fun for you. Like I don't know, dancing or wine-tasting or something. Call me."

Maybe it wasn't a bad thing I saw Justin in the alley of the Starlight. And here I'd thought the deputy was staring at me because I'd looked suspicious, or that he hated me for dating his friend. Justin wasn't Jackson. He wasn't jealous or controlling.

Maybe I could talk to him about Destiny being a murderer. Somehow, telling law enforcement that I saw a woman in a channeling session about to inject my ex-husband with something called "ehead um ide" didn't seem like enough evidence, or such a good idea.

I THOUGHT Rosalie was going to check my vital signs when she found out I'd spent all night doing a channeling with my awful dead ex-husband. She was the only person, other than Jackson, I could talk to about this; a fact that would have been comforting if it didn't feel like I was being clinically evaluated.

"How many hours do you think you were under Jackson's control?" she asked. She had a large black book opened in front of her with thick yellowed pages that looked like they were made out of some sort of animal hide. The Purple Pony had just opened and there weren't any customers yet, thank goodness. This book and her facial expressions were a little frightening.

"I'm not sure. It couldn't have been more than three hours," I said.

"Three hours?" she shot back like I'd said a million. "The longest I've ever heard of was an hour. One hour. And that person had to be hospitalized afterward." She looked me over. "You sure you're okay?"

I nodded.

"Three hours, huh?" she said again as she scanned the pages of her large book. "I hate to tell you this, honey, but that is not normal."

I laughed. "Like channeling with a ghost is ever normal."

She ignored my joke and continued in a softer tone. "This is very high-level stuff. Your mediumship is probably one of the strongest on record. It's beyond my scope or what I'm reading in any of these books. There has to be a reason you can connect with ghosts like this. Do you know anything about your parents, your biological ones, I mean?"

I tugged at the hangnail poking out on the side of my thumb. This was a sore subject, and one I didn't talk about too often. Any time I even tried to bring up my adoption with my mother, it led to "the face." "The face" was what I called my mother's hurt look: her cheeks lost their color, a soft weird voice took over her usual gruff one, her eyes half-closed into painful sad slits. It was such a difference in the person I knew to be my mother, I couldn't get myself to go into anything that caused the face to happen. So I told Rosalie the only answer my mother ever gave me whenever I got up enough nerve to ask.

"She doesn't know. It was a private adoption with a private lawyer. My biological mother doesn't want to be found or looked up. That's all she knows. Why?" The words came out in one breath. I hadn't meant to shout them, though.

Rosalie hugged me so hard her dangly earring caught in my curls. "Some things in life are harder than you think they're gonna be. So don't do them until you're ready, you hear?"

She hadn't heard me right. It wasn't my fear. It was my mother's, one of my mothers. Either my biological one or my adopted one, or both. They were the ones who didn't want me to discover this part of my life. Not me.

She didn't let go of her hug for a good thirty seconds. "I told Brock that same thing when he looked up his birth mother a few years back. You never know what can happen. He wasn't ready either, but he heard she was dying in hospice, so he went. Strung out, no teeth, no hair, literally rotting away. It broke his heart. Once an addict, always an addict. There might be a good reason this woman doesn't want to be looked up, or your adopted mother doesn't want you to look her up. You might have to be prepared for what you find, is all."

She was right. Some things were hard, and you needed to be ready for them. It was probably why I hadn't seen Tina yet. I wondered if I'd ever be ready for that, or looking up my birth parents.

Deciding to change the subject before I dug my hangnail out so far it bled, I told Rosalie about the amazing steak I'd eaten during the channeling and how everything smelled, tasted, and felt just like it would have if I were really experiencing them. "Only no calories," I said. "I highly recommend it for that reason alone. But then, the Starlight was a little awkward for those same 'way too realistic' reasons."

I had her mesmerized. She leaned over the opened book, her thick arms curling around the pages. "We are going to make a lot of money," she said, in the same tone I pictured P.T. Barnum using with Jo Jo. Still, I hoped she was right.

I told her about the road the Bowmans wanted to build through Gate Hill and the real reason they wanted the Victorian.

When I got to the part about Destiny, Candace, and Heather, I hesitated, stumbling over my words, stopping myself. Everything seemed to point to them in Jackson's poisoning that night, an attempted murder that was only halted because Jackson hadn't signed his papers yet.

These girls tried to kill Jackson. Period. That part seemed certain. What was still uncertain was how and why two out of three of them ended up in our yard. Had Jackson figured it out and retaliated?

I blurted out all the details before I had time to worry if I should mention them or not.

"So what are you going to do?" Rosalie asked me.

"I don't know yet. I can't tell the police I got my information from a channeling. They won't believe that and it'll just make me seem suspicious. I'm pretty sure I need Destiny to confess."

"That's not going to happen," she replied as the wind chimes on the door clanged together and our first customers meandered in, an older couple wearing designer everything.

"I have a plan," I said. She looked even more worried than before.

CHAPTER 23

READING BETWEEN THE LINES

I grabbed a shopping cart and threw my purse into its basket the next day, my head slumped awkwardly to the side to keep my phone up to my ear as I waited for my mother to pick up. A cool breeze blew through the parking lot along with the smell of diesel from the large trucks traveling through Landover to get to the more important cities. I pushed my cart through the automatic doors, pulling the list I'd written on an old receipt from my pocket:

Recorder, plain journal, mace, check the price of Swiss army knives (make sure they are sharp)...

"Hello honey," my mom said, answering. "How's the retail business?"

I tried to remember to keep my voice down. I had a tendency to yell when I was on my cellphone in a loud public place, especially when I was talking to my mother. "Great," I replied, ignoring her attempt to pick up where we'd last left off. "I was just calling because I want to know more about my adoption."

"What?" she asked.

I stepped to the side of the entrance to let other customers go around me and stuffed a finger in my ear. "I think it's time we talked about my birth mother and my adoption. I have a lot of unusual questions..."

The Walmart greeter smiled politely at me.

There was a long pause on the other end. My mother was talking to someone else in the room. "No. No. I put the margarita mix in the cabinet above the stove." Her voice was quickly back to the phone again. "Look, honey. Brenda's here. Can I call you back about this?"

Brenda was her best friend, and she was always there. They were rediscovering their youth, which meant they rented Redbox and went to happy hour together.

"No," I snapped then realized how loud I was being. I softened my tone. "There's always something. I'd like you to take a photo of everything you can about my birth, now while you're thinking about it, every document you have. I know you said I came with a blanket. I want a photo of that too."

No answer, just the rumbling sounds of the ice dispenser from her fridge spitting out ice. I knew I was being a buzz kill on her and Brenda's margarita night, but I didn't care.

Just the thought of margarita made the room spin a little. I leaned against my cart and continued. "It's important. Please tell me everything you remember. Right now on the phone. About the lawyer. About that day. How did you meet the lawyer? Where were you when you signed the papers? How did you get me?"

I felt "the face" over my phone connection. My mother was not happy.

"Carly Mae. This is not the time for this. Brenda and I rented a movie and I need to go. Besides, I've told you everything I can about your adoption. It was a closed and private

161

one. Your birth mother did not want to be found. Period. End of story. In fact, I'm pretty sure this is the very thing she was trying to avoid. So, in order to get you, I had to agree that I wouldn't discuss the details. I will send you all the documents I can *again*, though."

She'd never sent me a thing before. She only said that for Brenda's benefit and we both knew it.

"Stop lying," I said louder than I'd meant to.

She quickly said "good-bye" before I could say anything else. I knew she'd casually forget to send me anything, and then pretend later that she'd done it.

The old man in the dark blue vest sitting on the stool beside me tried not to give me a sympathetic look when I threw my phone in my purse and showed him the list. We both knew he'd been listening in.

"Hi," I said, pointing to the paper by his face. "Where can I find... let's see, a recorder, mace, and a really sharp Swiss army knife?" His eyes traced my face and my outfit. I could feel him mentally taking notes about my appearance to tell the police later if any adopted mothers happened to turn up dead. He was a bright man.

Later, in the parking lot of Walmart, I scribbled everything I could into the pages of the plain black journal. I was a writer. I could make this believable. I looked at the clock on my cell phone. It was already 6:30, and I hadn't even finished half a page yet. Thankfully, the library stayed open late on Fridays.

I still had Destiny's number in my phone from when she'd texted me during our drinking session in the alley that day, so I sent her a text:

Found Jackson's journal today. Interesting entry for March 18th. We need to talk. Call me.

I left it short and vague. It was better that way, more believable. I bit the tip of the pen as I tried to remember every detail I could for the diary pages. The injection. The way she tried to get Jackson to sign papers. The fact Candace and Heather were there with Jackson and Destiny on the night he'd been poisoned.

The details alone would be enough to bring authenticity to my project. And no one would have any problems believing my ex-husband kept a diary. He seemed like just the kind of narcissist who recorded every bowel movement. I made a mental note to add in a bowel movement for believability.

As soon as I finished, I threw my foot on the gas and headed over to the library. If I was going to make this ruse one-hundred-percent believable, I had to have a witness. I knew from the many click-bait articles I'd written over the last four years in my mother's basement that even the craziest of stories would be believable if you tied someone credible to the details.

Once again, I was the only person in there. "Sorry about the noise, Mrs. Nebitt," I yelled from the copy machines in the hallway by the bathrooms and the front door.

She didn't even shush me.

"I found Jackson's diary and I need to make copies of it because there's no way I'm giving Destiny Bowman the originals to Jackson's diary. That I just found. His diary."

She never looked up from her faded 1998 computer monitor, and I wondered if she even heard me.

I was just about to walk over to the counter and tell her how my murdering ex's death seemed suspicious when my phone rang. At least that got the older woman's attention. I looked down. Destiny was calling me back.

I rushed out the automatic doors without even saying

"good-bye" to Mrs. Nebitt (she didn't notice, I'm sure), cursing myself under my breath for not having the recorder I picked up at Walmart opened and ready for action. I should've known there was no way Destiny was going to text me back and leave a trail of evidence like that.

"Carly Mae?" she said in a sweet, calm voice. "What's this all about?"

"You know what this is all about." I tried to talk as slow as possible while fumbling with my key fob. I needed to get my recorder ready. I only hoped the woman wouldn't confess anything too damning until I was ready.

"I don't know what you're talking about."

I finally got my car door open. I ran my hand along the floor mats in the backseat, looking for my Walmart bag. "According to Jackson's diary, on the night of March eighteenth, you were in the VIP lounge with Candace and Heather. You were trying to get him to sign something."

Damn it. Why did I spill my beans so easily? If she confessed now, I was screwed.

There was a long pause where I pictured Destiny making "the face."

"You're lying," she finally said.

"Really? Here's an excerpt." I grabbed one of the pages of my fake diary, enunciating every syllable into my phone. *"Destiny picked up my arm and tried to get me to sign a paper, saying, 'Do you know how hard it was to get him here? I had to promise him a surprise.'"*

It was a good five seconds before her whispered voice said, "That is crazy. Did I tell you Jackson was going crazy there toward the end? If he really thought that's what happened, no wonder he killed those girls."

"I think this diary proves he didn't. He mentioned something about a syringe."

"Never happened. But, I want to see this diary. I get off work in ten minutes. Meet me in the back of the Starlight when you get a chance, alone. I'll be looking for you. Bring this alleged diary you're talking about."

She hung up, and I let myself stop searching for the stupid recorder. I rested my head on my steering wheel, listening to the sound of my breathing in the stagnant warmth of my car, trying to calm myself down.

Heather and Candace used to be the only two people who could connect Destiny to Jackson's death. And now they were dead. Jackson was dead too. And here I was, announcing I was the one person left who could make that connection. She wanted me to bring that diary, all right, so she could get rid of me and all the evidence in one fell swoop.

Was I really going to meet that killer in a dark alley alone with nothing but a little canister of mace and a recorder? I kicked myself for not looking harder for the Swiss-army-knife section.

CHAPTER 24

MESSAGES

$\mathcal{I}$t was dark when I pulled into the alley. I turned my radio down and listened to my wheels crunching through the pebbles and trash along the street. My heart raced and I found myself hitting the door lock a few times for no reason. The recorder was in my lap, ready to go, right next to the mace I'd bought. Still, I felt anything but prepared.

I was late. I knew I would be. The library was in Potter Grove and the Starlight was in Landover. I pulled up to the backdoor and grabbed my phone to let Destiny know I was there, so I would have a trail of my own evidence. I pulled my copied diary pages from the passenger's seat and placed them over my lap to cover the recorder and the mace.

The backdoor opened and I fully expected a large blonde with pigtails to sashay out in a tiny bathrobe, but it was Bobby Franklin, Shelby Winehouse's fiancee. He lit a cigarette and nodded to me.

"Hey Bobby," I said, reluctantly rolling down my window. "What're you doing here?" I bit my lip and cursed myself for asking such a dumb question. He was the bouncer on a smoke break. I was the one who needed to explain myself. I wondered if I should ask for Destiny or tell him some sort of lie. I wondered briefly if he was here to "take care of me."

"Actually, I was waiting for you," he said, and I almost screamed.

He looked up at the full moon, his face a pale hairy beach ball in the moonlight. I put my car back into drive with my foot on the brake, ready to take off if I needed to.

He reached into the zippered part of his windbreaker and I threw my foot on the gas, pulling forward, stopping when I saw in my rearview mirror that he was waving an envelope at me.

He sauntered back over to my car. "Jumpy much?" He chuckled, like he knew he was creepy and relished it. He held the envelope out to me. "I was asked to give this to you if you showed up out here. No clue what it is," he said, even though I hadn't asked if he'd opened it.

I pulled the envelope through the little opened slot of my window, the other hand on my canister of mace.

"Thanks," I said, my heart still racing.

He walked away, across the alley, not even caring what was in my envelope. His pace picked up as he made his way down to the next street over. Every three seconds or so, he'd look up at the moon. I looked too. It was just a moon.

I watched as he rounded the corner, tugging on his shirt like it was suddenly strangling him. I thought I heard howling as I rolled my window up. It was really getting weird in Potter Grove.

I realized I was holding my mace so tightly my palm hurt. I opened the envelope.

Don't text. Don't call. It's not safe. Meet me at Bear Rock Drive-In. We can talk there.

Bear Rock Drive-In went out of business probably 20 years before I ever stepped foot in this town. There was no way I was going there alone to meet the woman who attempted to murder my ex-husband.

Of course, he'd been her husband at the time, and I'm sure he gave her (along with plenty of other people) good reason to murder him, but something in the back of my mind wouldn't let me think she could do it. She probably wanted to tell me who the only other voice was in the VIP room that night, though. And I was guessing she had to be extra cautious about it.

I called Rosalie, just so someone would know where I was headed, in case I didn't make it back.

"What in the hell do you mean you're going to meet Destiny outside the Bear Rock?" Rosalie only cussed when she was upset. "Carly Mae, no. This is not a good idea."

"I know. But I think I've got Destiny scared. I'm pretty sure I can coax a confession out of her. I've got mace and..."

"You've lost your flippin' mind. You suspect this woman killed Jackson and then you're gonna tell me not to worry because you have mace."

"I don't think she killed Jackson, not because she couldn't, but because she wouldn't have unless he signed his paperwork. But I think she knows who did, and I think she wants to tell me, but she's afraid. Or maybe she killed him. I don't know," I said, or I tried to say. Rosalie was still yelling about mace and bad ideas, and hadn't heard me.

I hung up on her. She was right. But I was still going.

I pulled down the dark road to Bear Rock, which was just as remote as the one up to Gate House. No streetlights, no street signs, just some friendly dead trees and abandoned furniture along the way to let you know where your dead body would likely be tossed later.

The only thing left of the old drive-in quickly came into view as soon as I turned the corner, the snack shack. Destiny's convertible was right next to it just like she said. I thought about texting her, but her note said not to. Of course, it might've said not to because she wanted to kill me without there being too many traces back to her. I sat and watched her car, but I didn't see any movement.

After about half an hour of waiting her out, I decided to just drive by and see if anyone was there. I wouldn't even get out of the car. I'd just do a quick drive by to check.

I turned off the music and listened to the plinking sounds of gravel rolling through my wheel wells. I didn't see Destiny, or anyone, as I drove by her convertible. I clutched my pepper spray, and pulled my cell phone from my purse, punching in 9-1-1, ready to send if I needed to. I slipped the phone into my back pocket.

Pulling up next to Destiny's car, I looked over. I couldn't really see anything.

This wasn't good. And I got the sinking feeling that I was being set up, and Destiny had the upper hand. Every brain cell I had screamed at me to turn the car around. But I didn't listen. Instead, I waited, engine still on, doors locked, mace in my hand... checking in between the dark silhouettes of the nearby trees, checking for any signs of a setup. After waiting five full minutes, I peeked over at the car next to me, but it was too dark to see anything through both of our windows.

She probably had her seat reclined and was asleep in there.

I put my hand over my horn but then put it back down again. "Just leave and call the police, Carly," I said out loud. A great plan, except that the sheriff was Caleb Bowman. I'd have to explain way too much to that awful man if I went that route. A forged diary, a text to my dead ex-husband's stripper, a channeling, why we were meeting here... And all because the woman had fallen asleep?

It was a two-second run. Three steps. That's all. I'd run over, check, and run back. I kicked my car door open and ran to hers, tugging wildly on her door. It was locked. I knocked on the window then cupped my hands around my face and put my eyes as close to the window as I could. Not much, just a purse laying on the passenger's side seat. And a note, on the driver's side floor that I couldn't make out from this side of the car. I took a deep breath and ran over to the driver's side window, squinting into the darkness of her vehicle to read what it said:

Meet me at Canyon Rock Drive-In. Don't text. Don't call. I want to talk to you about something -- Carly Mae

I BARELY KNEW WHAT HAPPENED. The pain was immediate. No air. Something tight wrapped around my neck, choking me from behind. My vision fogged into darkness, and I tried to breathe but couldn't. I kicked wildly, but the thing around my neck got tighter, and tighter. I reached my hand behind me, running it up my back. Clamping my finger down as hard as I could while keeping my eyes closed, I depressed the mace button, spraying and spraying. Foam dripped down my own hand, tingling and numbing it instantly. But the noose-like thing around my neck that threatened to snap my bones loosened enough for me to breathe in a gulp of my own pepper spray. I didn't think. Coughing and hacking, I just ran straight ahead, not caring where I was headed or how I was going to make it back to my car. I took off to the only coverage around me, the snack shack. A lopsided, half-torn-down, pile of graf-fitied-up plywood that smelled like pepper spray. Everything smelled like pepper spray. My own eyes stung and watered so much I couldn't see. I didn't dare wipe them with my hand, though. I knew that would make things worse. I looked around. Noticing a board by my feet, I picked it up and swung it around to check every direction for whoever it was who had choked me.

Had Destiny been set-up too? Or did she just want me to think she'd been?

I rubbed my neck, fully expecting to feel blood or a bone jutting out or something. Everything ached and I could hardly swallow, but I seemed to be okay. Blinking through pepper-spray-induced tears, I looked in every direction, checking my surroundings but not seeing or hearing anything. Just those damned cicadas laughing at me in the distance.

I took a step forward. My car was still running, and my driver's side door was open, thank God. I needed to try to reach it. But, I suspected, Destiny (or whoever the strangler was) was watching my car too -- *or was hiding in it.*

Quickly, I reached in my back pocket for my phone that I'd already punched 911 into.

"Damn it," I muttered a few times when nothing was there. I must've dropped my phone somewhere in my run or while I was being choked.

I stared at my car, knowing it was my only hope.

I waited half a minute, until my eyes were clear enough to focus forward, and I knew I had a straight shot to Destiny's car, which was the only straight shot I could see. I mentally counted to three then took off to her passenger's side, still carrying the board at the ready to smack someone harder than they ever thought a woman my size could do.

I stopped and looked around then inched my way toward the back of her vehicle, checking in all directions the whole way, my nose dripping, eyes running. The fact I didn't see or hear anyone was not comforting. My heart thumped out the score from Jaws with each careful step I took. I tripped over something squishy yet lumpy, and I looked down. An outstretched hand under Destiny's car.

Screaming the rest of the way, I bolted into my own running car, locked the doors then smacked every inch of the back seat with the board. Only after I didn't feel or see anything did I throw my car into reverse and pull away. I'd watched enough horror movies to know I had to smack that back seat first.

I drove straight to the police station, wondering what on earth I was going to say to Caleb Bowman, especially with my name all over a note in a possibly dead woman's car.

The good news was I'd probably just cleared my ex-husband's name, but only because I'd thrown my own name under the suspicion bus.

I didn't realize I was still screaming when I rushed through the doors of the police station until Justin ran out from the back and asked me what was going on. I collapsed into his arms, surprised he let me.

Tears streamed down my face as I blurted it all out, telling him everything, yelling that Destiny needed help.

"I'll send an ambulance out to the drive-in and radio the sheriff," he said. "Caleb's patrolling that area right now. But I'm going to need to know exactly what happened out there and why in the hell you were meeting your dead ex-husband's widow at a deserted drive-in."

CHAPTER 25

AND THEN THERE WAS ONE

he news was full of Destiny's murder the next day. I knew I was to blame for it. Even though that woman had tried to kill Jackson and may have succeeded about a week later, this was something I would carry around with me for the rest of my life. I was responsible for taking someone's life. My dumb plan. My dumb lie. And I'd almost gotten myself killed over it too.

I pulled my blanket around my shoulders as I watched the news, and my hand accidentally brushed against my neck. A pain shot all along my neck bones, reminding me just how fragile life was.

Caleb was in the middle of another one of his press conferences, scratching at his beard dye, his beady eyes twitching as he talked into the mic. I wondered if he smelled like pepper spray too. He pointed to a reporter in the crowd.

The reporter shouted, "Is this a copy cat murder or is this the same killer?"

Caleb shuffled back and forth in front of the podium, his father by his side. He looked over at the mayor before he spoke. "At this point, we can't know either way. But it does have all the earmarks of a copy cat crime, certainly. It might not be related." He pointed to another reporter.

"Was she strangled like the other women?"

"Yes. This death has similarities to the other women, but it also has many differences, and we'll be examining all angles here in the coming weeks."

Jackson appeared on the couch next to me. I didn't jump even though I was surprised to see him so soon after our channeling. He didn't say a word, just looked at my neck, which had turned an even brighter shade of purplish blue since I'd checked it in the bathroom at the police station last night, bruise streaks across my throat in the shape of a rope or something. Jackson swept my hair away from my face like he used to do when we were married, except now it was like a cold brush of air. He never said a word, never blamed me for Destiny's death, even though I wanted him to.

"What happened?" he finally asked after a couple of minutes.

I told him everything I remembered about the channeling and the forged diary, the alley and the old drive-in, then waited for him to let me have it. I wanted him to let me have it, tell me how dumb I'd been, blame me for all of this.

Caleb was still babbling away, now about a couple "persons of interest" in the case. I knew one of them was me.

I was actually surprised they'd let me go home last night at the police department, to be honest. I'm not sure I would have let someone as suspicious as me go — dead strippers found in her yard after her ex-husband cheated on her with a stripper, then the woman her ex-husband cheated on her with turns up dead too, with a suspicious set-up note in her car. Yep, I would've convicted me.

We were down to one person being alive from the champagne room that night, and it was the only person Jackson was too drugged to see.

I could barely focus as I shuffled to the closet to find my puffer jacket, even though it was way too hot for it. It was the only thing I owned that zipped past my neck. My eyes fogged into tears thinking about how things had gone, how they were going. How I'd risked my life for people who were already dead, and who had, for the most part, been terrible to me to begin with.

And through it all, there was one good friend who'd needed a friend the most, and I'd pretty much ignored her. Because I couldn't handle my own guilt. I didn't have my GPS anymore because I didn't have my phone. But I remembered it was a 20-minute drive into Freemont, a town about the size of a mouse turd, and almost as pleasant.

"Where are you going?" Jackson asked when he saw me grabbing the jacket.

"Out."

"Someone just tried to kill you, and you decide it's a good time to go out for no reason?"

I zipped up my jacket, my armpits already sweating under its insulated fabric. "I'm pretty sure, at this point, I have a police tail."

TWENTY MINUTES LATER, I found myself driving up and down streets, looking for the boarding house. I remembered from my GPS it was called Safe Home and that it was on Garmont Street. I didn't know the exact address, but I guessed it was the only brick house on the block without rusty bikes propped up against weed-infested flower boxes. I took a deep breath and got out of the car.

The woman in the yellow teddy-bear scrubs was anything but sweet. She pursed her lips from behind the counter, staring at my neck, or so I felt. It might've been the puffer jacket I was wearing in July. "Visiting hours are between 7:30 pm and 9:30 pm only," she said.

Rats. I hadn't thought to call first. "Look, I came a really long way. Okay, twenty minutes, but still. I'm an old friend of Tina Carmichael's..."

The woman interrupted me with a wag of a finger and a tsking noise. "A patient's right to privacy is very important to us at Safe Home. Please refrain from using last names. Although I'm sure Tina C would be delighted to see you, visiting hours are restricted for a reason. Most patients hold jobs during the day or are in various therapies." She went back to her computer.

Security around here was oddly reminiscent of the strip place, and I didn't have a ten. "Can I write her a note, leave my number so she can call me?"

"You can write a note, but calling you back would be up to the patient."

I stared at her a second. "Do you have some paper?"

After a long sigh and a few more tsks, she stood up and went into the back room. As soon as she left, I quickly thumbed through the visitor's log that was sitting on the counter in front of me just to see who had come to visit Tina lately. Every once in a while I glanced up to check if scrubs-lady was back again. The walls were a stark, bright white with odd abstract splatter paintings adorning them. It was so clean, so bland...

Every part of me wanted to take off through the door of

the stupid lobby and yank Tina C out of whatever therapy she was involved with right now. Take her away from this sterile place, back to our dorm room with the mountain of crumpled tissues and soda cans strewn all over the place and our "Wall-O-Future" (mostly magazine cut-outs of European castles and tropical islands that we taped photos of ourselves into), and escape so she could be Tina Carmichael again. So we could be us again.

Checking the pages of the spiral notebook, I noticed Mrs Carmichael wasn't the only one who'd come by to see Tina. Rosalie had come two months ago and so had Shelby and Bobby (probably with Mrs. Carmichael), Brock a few months back, and even Justin. *Justin?* Was I the only one who never came? I felt even guiltier when I noticed not nearly as many people came to see Tina C as her roommate Tracey M.

Scrubs-lady strutted back through the door, her smile-scowl returning when she saw me thumbing through the pages of the notebook. She quickly snatched it from me, bringing it through the opening in the plexiglass partition so it was on her side now. Apparently, visitors had a right to privacy too. She handed me a piece of printer paper.

Her eyes seemed glued to my neck as she spoke, stuttering over her words. "I'll see that Tina C gets this, b-but like I said before, whether or not she calls you back is completely up to her."

As soon as I left, I pulled off my jacket and let myself enjoy the instant relief of not being smothered by a wearable sauna. Then I rummaged through my purse for my cell phone. Maybe Mrs. Carmichael could help me talk to Tina because I seriously doubted this place was going to give her any messages from the woman in the winter coat with the strangle bruises. After searching under my wallet and through my forged diary pages, I remembered I no longer had a cell phone and I didn't have any extra money to get it replaced either.

I walked out past my car and the small parking lot, searching for the vehicle I hoped would be there. It was. And it was easy to spot in this town. Justin had a thing for clean, shiny, not-even-one-piece-of-bird-poop vehicles. Clearly, he didn't know you shouldn't stand out when you're tailing someone.

He reached across the seat and popped the passenger-side door for me as soon as I got to his pickup.

"Just so you know," he said as I climbed into the seat next to him. "I'm following you around for your protection. I don't think you did anything."

His large brown eyes were sincere. Still, I didn't believe a word. "Great," I replied. "Then, you probably won't mind if I use your cellphone."

CHAPTER 26

UNSTABLE

*M*rs. Carmichael's voice always rattled a little when she talked like she was holding in a smoker's cough even when she wasn't. But today, it was particularly hard to hear her over the clanks and clatters of the many patrons eating lunch at Spoony's after church. Sundays were bratwurst.

I dug my toe into the soft grass along the curb in front of me, walking the sidewalk around Justin's truck, watching him be bored sitting in his truck without a cellphone. Every once in a while our eyes would catch and one of us would look away. It was always going to be awkward like this between us now.

"I gotta make this quick, Carly Mae," Mrs. Carmichael said after telling me how sorry she was about Destiny and everything. "I can't help you. They should've told you Tina's not accepting visitors right now. She's going through another rough patch. Honestly, I think it's her roommate. She's got a new one now and the girl's one of those Gordons from Landover. You know the ones who own the Volvo shop? I feel for the girl, but the whole family's loud and bossy. It's setting Tina off."

A gentle breeze blew through my curls, but it was still not enough to cool me down. Sweat dripped along my hairline and I wasn't even wearing the jacket anymore.

She continued. "The old roommate, I told you about her, Tracey M. She was quiet as a little bird." She paused like she might be thinking that through. "Probably because she's sick all the time. Hypochondria runs in her family, poor thing. You know Mrs. Moorehead, the woman at the pottery shop..."

I looked over at Justin, who was still staring at me. I gave him the one-minute sign. For a woman who had to make this quick, Mrs. Carmichael sure liked to talk.

That's when it hit me. *Did she just say Moorehead?* I no longer heard a word Mrs. Carmichael was saying. Moorehead ended in ehead. As in ehead um ide. The rest of the bottle from that night could easily have been Tracey Moorehead Potassium Chloride. It was a long shot but it might explain a lot.

"Did Tina's old roommate receive potassium injections?" I asked, practically shouting into the phone.

"Now how in the world do you think I'd know something like that? And why do you..."

I didn't let her finish. "Please, Mrs. Carmichael, please see if you can have Tina call me back as soon as possible. This is important."

"I suppose I could tell the center it's an emergency."

"Yes. Tell them that," I said. I lowered my voice as I walked back toward Justin's truck. "It's definitely an emergency."

He rolled his window down as soon I got back and I handed him his phone. He stared at my neck a second, squinting his eyes at me, like he was searching my bruises for some sort of long forgotten truth, probably hoping I'd offer up a confession.

I just let the awkward silence hang between us. I knew it was there for more reasons than the fact my answers had been purposely vague at the police station last night.

I knew there were also so many unspoken things between us in general.

Justin motioned for me to get in. "Since you're here, you wanna answer a few more questions about last night?"

"Nope, but thanks for the offer. I'm tired and my neck hurts. You gonna follow me home?"

He slowly nodded. A man of few words.

"Race you there," I said, walking away. I turned around. He was still staring at me. Maybe it was stupid. Maybe the pressing need to tell someone everything was laying heavier on my conscience than I thought. Or maybe I just trusted silent people way too much, even ones I'd slept with.

I turned back around and opened his passenger door again. "I confronted Destiny last night. I told her I thought she killed Jackson."

"Come on, Carly Mae," he said as I slid in. "Think of a better lie than that. Jackson died of a heart attack."

"That's not what he thinks." I bit my lip. I could hardly believe I was about to tell this guy all of this. "Rosalie and I had a seance."

He looked down at his perfectly polished black steering wheel. "If you're not going to be serious..."

"If you don't want to hear the truth, then don't." It wasn't exactly the truth, but I wasn't under oath, and exactly-the-truth was exactly too crazy.

"All right," he said. The slowness in his voice made it seem like hearing me out was probably going to be the most painful thing he had to go through today, worse than the bird poop I saw on the top of his truck. "Is this going to be a confession? Because I have to record it if it is."

"No. I didn't do anything." I slammed his truck door and leaned across his console. "I lied to Destiny, though. I took down notes from that seance and I pretended they were Jackson's diary. They incriminate her in poisoning Jackson a couple weeks before he actually died. She was going to inject him with potassium chloride."

"Going to," he said so I'd know that part was important. "But she didn't."

"She was sure scared last night when I read her an excerpt of the diary, though."

"I'm sure she was."

"She was," I said. "She practically begged me to meet her at the Starlight. Then, when I did, Bobby handed me that letter. Talk to Bobby. He told me Destiny gave him that letter to give to me. He set us up. I told you that last night."

"You and Bobby have conflicting stories."

"I bet. Because he's a liar."

I thought I saw him holding in a smile. "Anything else weird happen?"

"Yes. Bobby took off down the alley after he gave me the letter, looking up at the moon like it was chasing him. I think I heard him growling. I know that sounds crazy."

Justin looked out the window at the sky like he expected the moon might already be visible even though it was just afternoon. "You don't think he's a shapeshifter, do you?" he finally said in such a tone I knew he teasing me a little.

I opened the truck door again. I was done here. "But one more thing. Bobby was very interested in contacting the strippers during our seance. And," I paused for emphasis. "He told me if Shelby ever talked about working at the Starlight, he'd have issues. But he punched his fist into his hand when he said it."

Justin raised his eyebrows. "That really happen?"

"Yes. Everything I just told you really happened."

"You still have those diary pages? I'd like to see them if you do," he said.

I pulled them out of my purse and laid them on the seat. I could tell by the way he scanned my crumpled copied papers, this person-of-interest had passed her interrogation. It was likely Bobby's turn.

CHAPTER 27

NO AMBIGUITY

*I*t was already late by the time I started my long drive up Gate Hill, a drive that was not getting easier despite my practice. But somewhere around the second gate, it dawned on me exactly why I was making bad decisions in life, and risky plans. Exactly why I worked retail and was helping my ghost of an ex husband solve a murder that might not have happened.

I couldn't soar into my future because I was clinging too hard to my past. I needed to let things go, especially the annoying, snotty things that wanted me to solve their murders.

Jackson was in a bad mood that night when I got home. Or maybe I was. Much like when we were married, I couldn't tell the difference.

"How's our little investigation going," he said in a tone that was locked and loaded. "Find my killer yet?"

I threw my keys down on the counter, and shoved Rex's food in the microwave to heat it up.

"I'm too exhausted," I said. "We'll talk later, maybe." I

thought about the sage in the drawer, and how quickly I could move away from this part of my past.

IIis voice was strong and his color good, hardly any fading at all. He'd probably spent all day resting, like a bored 50-year-old without a job. He was always going to be here. I gasped a little in my head. *Was that how my mother felt when I was living in her basement?*

I rubbed my neck. I couldn't go back. That was my past too.

"Are you okay?" he asked.

"Go away." I ran upstairs and slammed the door to our old bedroom as he floated after me down the hall. "I said I'll talk to you tomorrow," I yelled.

As soon as I shut the door, he appeared, cross-legged on his favorite chair, staring at fingernails that didn't really exist. "Go to sleep then. I'll wait."

"Look," I said. "I know you think you're my Watson, and that we're somehow a team, investigating your murder case together, but you're not my Watson."

"Of course not. I would be the Sherlock. Just like I'm the Nancy. You're the Drew. I'm that curly haired British magician. You're my spunky sidekick I spend the first season pretending not to adore."

He hovered over the bed where I was sitting. He knew I had a thing for Jonathan Creek. And he was a far cry from that cutie.

He continued. "I'm actually surprised to see you. I thought you'd be out with what's-his-face. Your new friend called a bunch of times inviting you out."

"Brock," I said. "My *gorgeous* new friend has a name, Nancy. You know that."

"He should've called your cell."

"I don't have a cell anymore…"

The phone rang and I bolted down two sets of stairs to get it. The answering machine was just picking up and I raised my hand over the receiver but didn't grab it. What if it was Tina? I should have prepared something to say.

It was her. Her voice sounded weird to me, really high-pitched and overly excited, as she left her message. "So, my mom said I should call. You have an emergency or something? It's been a long time. My mom said to call. Come visit me next week if you're not worried… worried. The bear might come back. He told me *he wants to rip your tree limbs off, bury them with his blue shovel claws. Rip your fingers off. Bury them in shallow graves. With his blue… his claws…The king of hide-n-go-seek. The king of the forest.*"

I stared at the phone, unable to pick it up.

"What's the matter?" Jackson asked, motioning toward my hand that was still hovering over the receiver. "Don't you want to talk about playing hide-n-seek with the king of the forest? You don't see blue shovel claws every day."

"You're a dick," I said, picking up the phone, almost hoping I wouldn't catch Tina in time.

I didn't. I got nothing but a dial tone. I'd missed my chance tonight to ask Tina about her roommate, to tell her about Brock, to reconnect. After listening to her message, I wondered if that was even possible. I thought Mrs. Carmichael had been exaggerating that Tina was having a rough patch. Obviously, she hadn't been.

There were other messages already on my machine, and I played them back, ignoring my awful ex husband hovering nearby who I was growing more and more tired of. *Who was he to make fun of someone with mental issues? Who were any of us?*

The first one was Brock. "I heard what happened… Why

haven't you called?" he said in that nervous-boy tone I liked so much. I glanced over at Jackson. He was mimicking him. I turned away from the childish, old-man ghost who was never going to leave. The part of my past that was clinging to me.

Brock went on. "Anyway, I know this is terrible timing, but I forgot I have to leave for the weekend, some lame training event about new equipment we're upgrading to." He paused. "Hey, why don't you go with me? That would be fun. Plus, I don't think you should stay by yourself. I have to leave soon. So call me back as soon as you get this. I really think you should go. You should get away from this place."

I guessed the other three messages were him, too.

I reached for the phone.

"You're not seriously considering going with him, are you?" Jackson said. "You're safer here. You have a police tail now... Besides, you deserve someone with a semblance of a brain cell."

"Like you?" I yelled, punching in Brock's number as I made my way to the credenza in the back of the dining room. "Newsflash, Casper, you don't have any semblance of any brain cells anymore." I threw open the top drawer and sifted through the bills I'd stuffed in there.

If I was ever going to be Just-Carly, and move into the future, I needed to do this.

Brock didn't answer, but I left a message. My voice was almost defiant. "Not sure if you've already left yet. I hope not because I would *love* to go with you. Call me back as soon as you get this."

"I'm sure he's long gone," Jackson said as he sat back on the couch and put his shadowy legs up on the ottoman. "That message came in hours ago."

I pulled the sage out of the drawer and the lighter. "Why didn't you tell me when I first got home?"

"I'm not your secretary. Check your..." he stopped when he saw what was in my hands. I lit the sage. Pot-smelling smoke lifted up around me, making me wonder for a second if Rosalie had given me the right stuff. I waved it around myself, just like she told me. "You know, I used to think I was the immature one who needed to grow up in our relationship. Now, I know it wasn't me."

Jackson sat frozen, face contorted. His fear, his fading... I knew instantly the sage was going to work. This was my ticket to finally being me. I tried to remember Rosalie's instructions.

There can be no ambiguity. You have to tell the apparition to leave and mean it.

No problems in that department. "Jackson Bowman, you are no longer welcome in this house. You need to leave. Now."

His once darkened frame faded to a see-through light gray. I thought I heard him say, "Sometimes my jokes aren't funny. I'm sorry about making fun of Tina..."

"Jackson Bowman, you are no longer welcome in this house, and you need to leave now." I moved closer with the sage, waving it toward him, watching as he faded, lighter and lighter. I gulped but continued, circling the sage over the doorways and around the room, walking closer and closer to my soon to be future. "Jackson Bowman, you are no longer welcome in this house, and you need to leave now. Jackson Bowman, you are no longer welcome in this house, and you need to leave now." His voice was a whisper, but I thought I heard him say he loved me. His biggest joke so far. "Jackson fucking Bowman. You heard me. You are no longer welcome in this house and you need to move on."

He disappeared. I stood and watched the sage bundle still smoking in my hand, my eyes tearing up from the smoke, or so I told myself. The room felt empty. And it occurred to me it was.

I hadn't heard Rex all night.

"Rex!" I called, whistling. It was time to celebrate, only I didn't actually feel like celebrating. It was more just a sense of calm. Ash fell onto my shirt and I realized I was still holding hot sage. "Rex," I yelled again as I ran the sage to the the sink, listening for the sound of claws scraping along the hardwood, or a cocky ghost too stubborn for sage to work on him. Odd how I didn't hear either.

All the lights went out.

CHAPTER 28

SHOVELS

*A*fter trying several light switches and getting no responses, I stumbled back into the dining room to look for a flashlight, knowing full well what was causing my electricity problems, a pissed-off apparition who didn't like sage. "Look, I just need my space for a while. Maybe we can make an arrangement if we're going to live together..." My voice trailed off. Something didn't seem right. "Jackson?"

A clanging and a thud came from the kitchen. "Stop scaring me." I yelled this time. "Rex?"

No one responded. Maybe it wasn't Jackson or Rex. Maybe it was the house and the curse. "Look, Mrs. Harpton, I'm sorry I keep messing up on taking care of the house. I was already planning on being extra clean next week."

I pulled open the credenza and rummaged through the dark piles of papers there, where the sage was just moments ago, until my hand found the flashlight. I flicked it on and scanned the room. If we really did trip the circuit breaker, I'd have to go down to the basement to flick it back on.

The thought made my heart jump into my throat. Just like

the turret, the basement had an odd entrance, and its own set of spooky problems. I took a deep breath, reminding myself I was 31 years old. I could fix this situation, which was just a tripped circuit. And the noise was just Rex.

Still, I practically ran to the kitchen and threw open the cabinet that held all the keys on little nails. Going to grab the basement one, I noticed for the first time that the key to the turret was missing. *Had I forgotten to put it back when I went up for the internet a few days ago?*

I yanked the basement key from its hook and closed the cabinet, catching a glimpse of a dark figure out of the corner of my eye. "Jackson?" I said, my voice shaking.

The cabinet with the keys was in the part of the kitchen nearest the dining room and I backed farther away from it, toward my car keys by the microwave and the exit to the veranda. I swung the flashlight around the room as I walked backwards. I no longer thought it was a tripped circuit. But I could still get back to my car if I could get to those keys.

I ran my hand along the tiled countertop by the microwave, never taking my eyes off the beam of light from my flashlight as it moved all over the kitchen. I didn't feel my keys. Instead, right where I thought my keys should have been, my hand brushed against something small, rectangular, and smooth. A cell phone. I'd gripped that plastic case so many times, my hand instantly recognized it as my own. The one I'd lost when I discovered Destiny's body. Whoever was there that night wanted me to know they were back.

The only person who could possibly have put that there... probably also had my car keys right now, and was standing just inside the doorway shadows.

I rushed out the back door, the cool night air hitting my face. The cicadas sounded especially loud tonight, the air thick with humidity. I jumped off the veranda, not even bothering with the stairs. But I had no idea where to go from there. I couldn't run all the way down Gate Hill, not with a killer on my tail. I needed to figure things out.

I ran the list of suspects through my mind. Caleb? Bobby Franklin? Where was my police tail when I needed him?

Something Tina said stuck with me more than anything else.

Rip your fingers off. Bury them in shallow graves. Blue shovel claws...

What I took as the ramblings of a crazy woman... what the entire town thought was the ramblings of a crazy woman... was really a woman sharing with us the reason she went over the edge.

She really saw something that night. Four years ago just before her first episode. Jasmine Truopp. It must've set her off.

And with that thought, I knew who it was. My stomach lurched. Why had it taken me so long to figure things out, to do my good friend right for once?

The sound of tires crackling along dirt and rocks broke the silence. I was never happier to hear it. Still, it might take half an hour for whoever it was to get up that hill.

I ducked behind my car and waited, keeping an eye on any movement in the house, scanning the dirt around me for a weapon. I didn't have many options: a totally-dried-out, brittle tree branch or a couple of medium-sized rocks too large to do anything except toss underhandedly at the killer. I thought about Rex. Rex was probably held up in the turret, which had to be why the key was missing. I knew, as old as that dog was, he'd help me if he could.

That's when I saw it, the dark figure standing on the

veranda against the wall in the shadows, right by the opened door to the turret. Damn it. He was waiting for me to try to find Rex.

Smarter than Jackson ever gave him credit for.

The tire sounds grew louder. I thought I saw a gun in the silhouette of the killer on my porch. My guess, he was also wearing his blue-shovel claws, just like Tina said.

His work gloves.

CHAPTER 29

UNEXPECTED GUESTS

I wasn't one-hundred percent sure I was right, but it was worth a shot. "It's over, Brock," I said. "Some-one's coming up the hill. It's gotta be Justin. You'd better get out of here."

The figure didn't move, probably thinking it through. I went on. "Wondering how I knew, huh? Probably didn't think I'd figure it out."

My nose ran, and I wiped it with my sleeve, catching the faint smell of sage and pepper spray still lingering on my fingers. "You said the last time you visited Tina was last year, but that's a lie. You visited her in March, right before Jackson died of a heart attack. You probably visited every time that poor girl went off."

He didn't move, and I questioned whether or not I was right.

I went on. "Tina's old roommate was Tracey Moorehead. Remember her? A woman with mineral deficiencies? Got your hands on some potassium chloride, huh? Such a great idea to get Destiny to go along with things. She needed a rich husband to change his will and die before he noticed the changes. And you needed a dead pervert to take the fall for some murdered strippers. I'm gonna guess Destiny didn't know that last part."

I could hear the engine now, not just tires kicking up pebbles. *Thank Goodness.* Justin was almost here. My voice grew to a whole new smug level. "Great plan until Destiny let it slip that I'd found Jackson's journal... and that journal spelled out everything including the potassium chloride you stole from Tina's roommate. You panicked and decided it was time to get rid of the only people who could trace anything back to you — me and Destiny."

Headlights bounced into view. I ran toward them. It wasn't Justin. It was Rosalie. *Rats.* Waving my arms wildly through the air, I tried to motion to her that she shouldn't turn the car off, that we needed to leave. She seemed to be in a hurry too, pulling right up to the house, barely stopping before she kicked open her door. I yanked wildly on the passenger's side. It was locked.

Rosalie didn't seem too concerned with my theatrics. She wiggled her bad hip out. "Honey, thank goodness you're already out here, ready to go. Where have you been and why's it so dark? I've been calling all night," she said. She was wearing her seance dress, the sleeveless gray one with the moons. "Now I know you've been through a lot, so if you don't want to do this seance, I completely understand. Just remember Suzie is a high-paying..."

I ran over to the driver's side and pushed on the thick of her arm, attempting to shove her back into her car. "The killer's here. We need to go. Now. Get back in. It's Brock," I whispered.

"Brock?" she yelled. "My nephew? A killer? Are you crazy?

I'm just gonna use your bathroom then we'll head back down the hill. Stop kidding around."

I shoved her arm harder. "Just turn the car back on. Hurry. I'll explain later," I looked up. We were staring at a masked figure with a gun.

"Oh Lord," she said, holding her hands up.

"Brock, you don't have to do this," I said, mostly because that's what everyone says at a time like this. I actually knew killing us was his only way out.

He yanked the flashlight from my hands, never taking his mask off, never confirming our fears. He just motioned for us to go inside, probably so he could think things through, get up enough guts to kill us. I knew Rosalie was the part that made this hard for him.

I sat down on the sofa next to her. The dim light streaming in from her headlights was the only thing lighting the room besides Brock's flashlight. "Brock, I know all about your birth mom, how she was a prostitute and an addict. And I understand. You were angry. You were the bear in Tina's psychotic episode, biting people's limbs off."

"Stop saying that's Brock," Rosalie snapped.

The dark figure sat down on the settee across from us, never letting the gun down, like he wanted me to continue. He wanted to know how I knew.

"It came to me when Tina called me back. She kept saying weird things about bears tearing off fingers, burying things. I think she witnessed at least one of the attacks. Probably the first lady to go missing, the prostitute, Jasmine Truopp four years ago. Around Tina's first episode at the Shop-Quik."

Rosalie smoothed out her dress even though nobody cared about dress wrinkles.

"Psychotic episodes are triggered by trauma sometimes. I

heard that," I said to Rosalie. "From Caleb, but it's probably true. The blue shovel claws are his work gloves. He gave Destiny the sodium chloride from Tina's roommate to use on Jackson. Probably the GHB too. If you check the records at Safe House, I bet you'll find every time Brock visited Tina, she had an episode. And those episodes happened whenever Brock wanted to make sure his star witness was still too crazy to be credible."

Rosalie stood and held her hand up like she was going to slap me. She sat back down again. "Stop it," she said, her voice quaky, and even in the dim light of the flashlight, I saw her eyes were full of tears. "So Brock visited Tina? Big deal. That does not mean he caused her episodes, or that he stole potassium whatever from the halfway house and killed women." She turned to the man in the baggy sweatshirt with the gun held to us. "He doesn't even look like Brock." She stood up. "I should rip that mask off myself. That's what I should do."

"Please don't," I said.

Rosalie lifted her hand over the figure like she was actually going to remove the killer's mask, and I saw my chance to go for the phone. In one fluid movement, the figure smacked Rosalie across the head with the butt of his gun without saying anything. She fell to the floor, and he stared at her a second, probably to make sure his aunt was still breathing, while I put the receiver up to my ear. It was my one chance. But there was nothing but silence.

Of course, a cable guy would know to kill the communication lines first.

I tried to drop the phone before he saw me, but he turned, and I screamed.

"I didn't want to do this, Carly Mae," he said, yanking his mask off.

I looked down. I really didn't want to be right. I really wanted it to be Bobby or Caleb or Justin or even the neck-tattoo guy from the Starlight.

But in the darkness of the living room, I saw it was Brock.

He jerked the phone cord out of the wall with one tug then pulled his aunt's limp arms behind her back and wrapped the cable around them again and again. "I don't want to do this, but I have to."

CHAPTER 30

A CROOKED MAN

*B*rock's movements were jerky and quick. It was as if he needed to talk himself into killing me before he lost his nerve. "I don't want to do this," he said, over and over like a malfunctioning robot as he paced the rug in the living room. The beam from his flashlight bobbed all around the dark walls and floor as he gestured. "But I have to. Have to do this." He was sputtering now; spit flew from his lips as he argued with himself.

The smell of sage still lingered in the air, reminding me how dumb I'd been. *Why had I forced Jackson to leave?*

"My mother was a filthy whore," Brock went on. "A filthy whore like the girls in the clubs. And they deserved what they got."

His voice was tense, like he was mumbling through gritted teeth. "My own mother left me in the back seat of her car as a baby while she turned tricks. It was all in the police report and my adoption papers. All right there."

At least you have adoption papers, was what I was thinking. I didn't say that, though. I just hoped Brock would keep talking until my police tail got there. Where was Justin anyway?

"I went to see that whore four years ago when she was dying..." His voice raised and lowered unnaturally as he talked; the veins in his neck throbbed. "To forgive her. She didn't even say she was sorry. You know what she did? She begged me, on her death bed, to call her dealer and buy her some meth. She'd already lost her fingers. And she wanted me to sneak her drugs? She didn't say she was sorry. I gave her the chance and she only cared about herself."

"So you took it out on Jasmine," I said.

He shook his head. "I took it out on a whore. I should've killed Tina too. She saw me outside the Shop-Quik. I told her if she told anyone, I'd bite her fingers off, tear her limbs off like the rotting limbs of my mother..."

He looked all around the room, but stopped when he reached me. "I'm sorry we didn't get to have sex, Carly Mae," he said. I tried to keep my eyes from bugging out, but I honestly hadn't expected him to say that. I somehow held in my shock and my throw-up.

"We should've had sex. You would've liked it." He looked over at his aunt. "Sorry you had to hear that, Aunt Rosalie."

Her unconscious body didn't answer him.

"Let's go," he said, grabbing my arm, yanking me to my feet. He raised the gun to my temple. "There's still time to make those dreams come true."

He pulled me toward the stairs, but stopped at his aunt's side. Through gritted teeth, he mumbled, "She's my girlfriend, Aunt Rosalie. It's okay."

I gulped, and he turned back to me. "Move. Up the stairs."

I couldn't believe this was happening. I bit my lip, telling myself to remain calm. Maybe I could catch him off guard if I went along. Maybe I could get the gun. I needed to get the gun.

Yanking my arm hard, he pulled me up the two flights of stairs to the floor with the bedrooms, pushing me past the room with the blackbird wallpaper and down the hall toward the main one. "Tell me how much you love me and beg for your life."

He didn't give me time to say anything. He pushed the gun hard against my head. "Don't make me wait," he said.

"Please don't kill me. I love you," I said.

"Good," he replied. "That's the way we're going to play this game. I tell you to do something, and you do it. No waiting."

He tossed the flashlight and pushed me down hard onto the chair by the door, shoving his pants' zipper in my face, pointing the gun to my head. I could see his sinister smile in the light from the full moon. I kept my eyes focused on his smile. On the moon.

But I sat, motionless.

He lifted my hand and put it on his zipper. "I said no waiting," he said, waving the gun around now.

I tried to get my fumbling fingers to unzip his pants, my eyes on the gun. That's when I noticed the dark shadow behind him.

"Well, this is an awkward 'I told you so,'" a very cocky voice said from behind the man with his crotch in my face. I blinked hard. I'd never been happier to see my awful dead ex-husband in my life.

He hovered by Brock. "I would've been here sooner, but somebody did this sage smudging thing..."

"Jackson," I said, my eyes avoiding Brock's unzipped pants, and the fact he wasn't wearing underwear.

Brock turned his head toward the back of the room. "Who

in the hell are you talking to? Your dead ex? You goin' crazy like your friend?"

Seeing my chance, I kicked him hard in the crotch at the same time Brock's zipper flew up mysteriously, full speed ahead, catching along the extra sensitive parts of his flesh and tangling some of it into its teeth. Brock immediately grabbed himself, his face growing to a level of beet red I didn't know you could see in moonlight. He dropped the gun on his way down to his knees. I wasted no time picking it up and pointing it at him.

"Bitch!" he mumble-screamed, looking only at his darkening skin, half tangled in his zipper.

I stood over him, holding the gun with both hands, smiling smugly, taking full credit for his pain even though I'd had a little help.

He leaned on the chair to get up, still fiddling with his zipper.

"Don't get blood on my dead ex's favorite chair." I said, waving the gun toward the door. "Now, move. Downstairs." I still had to figure out how to restrain this guy, and more importantly, how to call the authorities. My phone cord had been yanked from the wall, my electricity was cut, and I had no idea where Rex was or my car keys. I took a deep breath. I could do this.

He didn't move. Through dark cheeks, he grinned. "You think it's really loaded, huh? All the other girls did too. I wasn't sure that was going to be the case when I followed those first two home from their work that day. But once they saw the gun, they just walked right into a masked stranger's car. A rental even. People see a gun and they think they don't have options."

I pulled the trigger, aiming right for his junk. It clicked, but nothing happened.

"Wow. You were really going to do that." He laughed, reaching for the gun. I kicked him hard in the junk and threw the gun at him as he toppled down forward, screaming obscenities at me. I've never run down two flights of stairs faster. I took off through the living room and out the kitchen door into the night. Rosalie's beams shown in an unhelpful direction as I looked around the veranda for what to do next.

"It's scary when you suddenly realize you don't have the power you thought you had, isn't it?" I heard him yelling from the house. He was getting closer.

I ran for the opened turret door. Maybe Rex was in there. Maybe my police escort, Justin, would finally show up soon. Maybe Brock wouldn't see me running into the turret and would look all around the yard, giving me time to find my keys, or Rosalie's. There were way too many maybes for me to feel comfortable about my odds. Still, I had to go with them. I knew Jackson was probably too weak to help me any more.

I heard Rex whimpering as soon as I ran in. He was gagged and chained to the couch in the room with all the paintings. Thankfully, he wasn't hurt. I tried to unhook him as heavy footfalls hit the wood of the veranda. I stopped frozen, chain in my hand, hoping Brock hadn't heard it rattle.

"Olly olly oxen free," he yelled into the night in a sing-song voice. He laughed. "If you're waiting for Justin, he ain't coming. I talked to him earlier tonight. Seems something you said had him convinced Bobby Franklin was the killer. He's tailing Bobby Franklin... can you believe it? Because the poor guy wants you to be safe. That's about the sweetest thing I've ever heard. I think that boy still likes you."

While he was talking, I managed to unhook the chain from Rex's collar. He shook his head a little too loudly in gratitude, and Brock stopped talking. The footfalls came toward the turret's entrance, faster than I expected. With no other option, I ran up the stairs to the library, Rex right behind me.

"Stupid, stupid, stupid..." he said, throwing open the door. It crashed against the back wall. "You're trapped. And all because you wanted to save your stupid dog. He's too old to help you and if he even tries, you'll be watching me kill him first."

I heard Brock checking through the paintings in the bottom room, throwing things around, probably to see if we were hiding there. I locked the library door and ran behind the desk chair.

Brock was soon on the stairs, clomping loudly so I'd know he was coming. Slowly.

My heart pounded so hard I felt it in my ears; my lip twitched unnaturally. I grabbed a couple books, but I knew they weren't going to do much. In the dim moonlight streaming in through the windows, I saw the library's knob move. I held my breath, making one last desperate attempt to find something of use besides some books. The desk drawers were locked. I knew that, but I still checked.

The door flew open with the kick of Brock's combat boot, and I screamed. Rex growled and moved forward, toward the killer, baring his teeth. My hero.

"You're a good boy," Brock said. "You remember me, right?" He put his hand out and my dog went to him, sniffing it. *So much for heroes.* Brock looked at me and smirked just as Rex bit into his hand, hard.

Yelling obscenities, Brock kicked my dog across the room. Rex smacked into the back wall, flopping down limp and lifeless. I screamed and crawled over to him, watching as Rex quickly rolled over, got up, and ran back to Brock, snarling.

Brock laughed harder. "You want some more, huh? Too stupid to know when to give up. Stupid runs in this family, I see." He kicked his boot through one of the stain glass windows adorning part of the back of the room. Glass shattered onto the ground below, clinking and clanking. "How 'bout I throw you out this window? First you, then your owner."

The room began to rumble, low and slow at first like the veranda when Mrs. Harpton was sweeping it. Then the whole turret shook, violently. Books soared from their places on the shelves, papers and pens flew from the desk, all the drawers opened now; everything pelted Brock on the head and back.

"What the?" he said, swatting the books away, trying to protect himself from the attack, backing up toward the opened window. His voice cracked as he spoke. "What in the hell is going on? As soon as this earthquake stops, I swear you're gonna get it."

"Earthquake? This is no earthquake and it's not going to stop," I said, matter-of-factly. "My house doesn't like you."

"You're crazy."

"That's right," I said, chucking my own books at him now, moving in closer to the man at the window. "I am crazy. And you should know not to mess with crazy."

Brock's feet lifted from the hardwood, setting him off balance. He swung his arms wildly around, trying to regain control, trying to comprehend just what in the hell was happening. "You bitch."

"It's just Carly now," I said, kicking him as hard as I could out the window, surprised when he teetered on the edge a second, swinging his arms around before falling. A loud thud soon followed, and even though I knew there was no way he could've survived that fall, I still checked. Every horror movie I ever watched made me know I had to check.

I turned toward what I thought was going to be a mess in the room. Everything was back in its place, books on their shelves, paper and pens back in the desk. I sat down on the chair and put my head in my hands. Rex came over and licked my arm. And I hugged him hard. "My knight in shining armor," I said.

One of the drawers of the desk was still open, and I couldn't help but think the house wanted to show me something or tell me something, which was crazy, except completely realistic all at the same time.

There was only one thing in the drawer, a large book with a gold embossed title: There Was *a Crooked Man*.

I STILL NEEDED to catch my breath and check on Rosalie, but instead, I found myself opening the book, barely able to see it properly in the darkness of the room. It was a scrapbook of sorts with old tattered black-and-white photos glued into its pages. Children in what looked like a classroom setting, the girls in perfect curls and white dresses, the boys in black uniforms. All sitting at tiny desks. Two adults stood off in the back. A man with a handlebar mustache and a woman in a high-collar black dress.

I squinted. *Was that Ronald and Mrs. Harpton?* It was a pretty fuzzy photo and the thought was impossible. Mrs. Harpton had to be this woman's great granddaughter. Either that or Ronald and Mrs. Harpton were some sort of ghosts that seemed an awful lot like real people. I held the photo closer. I just couldn't tell. It probably wasn't them.

I'd need to look at this later. A breeze from the broken window reminded me I shouldn't be doing this now, anyway.

I skimmed through the rest of the book quickly before closing it. Blackbirds and lewd old photos, kind of like this book was Playboy's creepy old grandfather. Sepia-toned, black-and-white images of beautiful young women in various stages of being undressed.

What on earth made me think the house wanted to show me this?

I shook my head, disappointed with myself for taking so much time for nothing, for believing my house had a message for me. I still needed to check on Rosalie, find her keys, and get help.

I was just closing the book when the last photo caught me by surprise. Three men stood around the very desk I was sitting at right now. I could tell from the stained glass windows in the background and the fountain pen sitting off to the side.

One of the men in the photo had round, Theodore-Roosevelt glasses and a buttoned-up, stuffy vest. I recognized him from other family photos. It was Henry Bowman, the designer of this house and Jackson's great grandfather. He was the only one in the photo I recognized, though. All three of the men were laughing, staring up at a woman dancing on the desktop in front of them wearing nothing but a single strand of long white pearls and some heels. I closed the book and pinched my arm, rolling the skin between my fingers until it stung under my touch, momentarily worried Mrs. Harpton, Ronald, and I had more in common than I thought.

That naked dancer looked just like me.

CHAPTER 31

CURSES

*T*ina and I reminisced the whole drive over to the cemetery the next week, talking about the food fights we used to get into in the back of the Thriftway, and the boyfriends we made up so we wouldn't seem pathetic, not realizing that probably made us extra pathetic.

She seemed stable now, looking over at me from the passenger's seat, her loose strings of blonde hair falling out of her ponytail and onto her round face. I knew things would never be like they were before her diagnosis, but little by little, they would still be okay.

I tried not to bring up Brock in case it upset her or Rosalie, who was sitting in the back seat of the car, but I told her if she was ever ready, I'd help her write a book about everything.

"My mother will be thrilled to hear I'm finally using my million-dollar English degrees for something," I said.

When we got to the cemetery, my heels poked into the plush dark green lawn like they were trying to touch the dead folks laying just underneath us. Not sure why I chose to wear heels, or Jackson's favorite dress.

OVER MY DEAD HUSBAND'S BODY

But then, my choices in life always did seem to rest on the edge of questionable.

Rosalie pointed to a batch of headstones to our right and we headed over there, my ridiculous heels squishing the whole way over. I scanned the gravestones, genuinely surprised none of these people were trying to communicate with me right now.

Tina handed me one of the bouquets of flowers we bought when I picked her up from Safe Home. Peonies and sunflowers, Jackson's favorite mixed with mine. Much like the dress and the heels, I wasn't sure why I chose that combination; it just seemed fitting. I hadn't seen my ex-husband since he helped me kill Brock about a week ago when we solved his murder, so I thought I should come say goodbye, maybe finally figure out where he was buried, and "pay my respects," so to speak.

Turns out, the Bowmans had a special area of Potter Grove Cemetery dedicated to them with its own gate and everything. Money had its privileges even in death.

"You think Jackson's really moved on?" Rosalie asked.

"I don't know," I said. "He said he would if I solved his murder."

Henry Bowman's headstone was next to his wife's and their four children. Since Jackson was an only child, he was there by his parents. Oddly, there was a blank tombstone with no words mixed among the various Bowmans.

"The unmarked grave," Rosalie said, pointing to it. "They say it's for all the women and children the Bowmans put through hell and high water to get where they got in life. Henry Bowman had the blank headstone put there, right on the other side of him so he'd never forget."

I nodded. I didn't tell her I thought it might've been for

Eliza. I hadn't shown her the photo or the scrapbook that I'd found in the drawer. I also didn't tell her how my Amytiville Horror house helped save us that night either. The poor woman had been through enough, learning that her nephew was the Landover stripper murderer.

I stared at Jackson's grave for a minute, thankful I didn't have to have his body exhumed after all. Thankful for a lot of things, actually. I put the flowers by his headstone and stood back to examine them.

A breeze blew my sundress up, and I barely grabbed it in time before my legs were exposed.

"My favorite dress for a reason," a voice behind me said. "And my favorite flowers, too? You do care."

I turned around. Rosalie and Tina had their heads bowed like they were praying.

"How in the world did you get here?" I whispered to the bearded ghost behind me. "I thought new apparitions could only manifest in the house."

"Looks like I've leveled up," he said.

I turned to see if Rosalie had heard me talking to the air. She looked up and winked then pulled Tina by the arm. "You said your dad's grave is here someplace? Let's go find it. Give him the flowers we brought," she said, leading Tina over to the sprawling hills sprinkled with gravestones.

For a minute, Jackson and I just stood there, not saying much. My long curls seemed heavy along my neck and I pulled them up into a bun. My bruises were still visible, but they didn't hurt as much anymore.

"I'm learning a lot about what it means to be dead," he finally said. "Things I should've learned while I was living."

He was a pale washed-out version of himself, like an image fading into the background as he hovered over the graves in his family's little gated community. I felt close to him, closer than I ever did when we were married. It was strange but familiar all at the same time.

"Thanks for helping me with Brock," I said. "With the zipper, and the... everything."

"Hardly worth mentioning," he replied. "I noticed."

I chuckled. I was glad the sage hadn't worked that night, and not just because he helped me. I would honestly have missed him. It made me realize maybe I didn't need to escape my past to move on to my future. Maybe, they were actually working together somehow to give me everything I needed to live the moment I was in. "I hate to admit it, but you were right about Brock."

I could see him smirking. I tried not to care.

"But for the record," he began. "Brock and Destiny did not murder me. They may have tried, but they did not succeed."

I rolled my eyes. "Because they weren't bright enough to murder someone as smart as you?"

"One can hardly argue with logic."

"They clearly tried to poison you once. I'm sure they just succeeded the second time. Either that, or you really had a heart attack. Old men who love strippers and alcohol often die from that, you know? Fire and brimstone."

He changed the subject. "I got a lot of paranormal messages on our way over here today."

I pulled a heel out of the soil. "It's weird I didn't. You'd think a strong medium walking through a graveyard would pick up on a ton of activity."

"I intercepted a lot of messages, so you wouldn't have to."

I patted my heart. "You *are* my secretary."

He ignored me. "Pretty much every murdered ghost within a hundred-mile radius wants you to solve their cases now using your channeling abilities. I'm not exactly sure why. I told them you failed to solve mine."

A couple meandered nearby with flowers and a tiny flag. So, I lowered my voice. "How on earth do they even know I solved these murders? You guys have some sort of phone?"

"Paranormal messages, and even spirits, can travel on the living. It's how I got here. I travelled on you."

Great. Now, in addition to being a medium, I was also some sort of ghost taxi and message service. It wasn't going to be long before I spit out ectoplasm; I knew it.

Jackson continued. "I told them they had to make it worth our while to do a channeling. We aren't running a nonprofit over here."

"Our while? You mean my while. I can't imagine what a ghost would have that would make solving their murder worth my while, though."

"What about knowledge? Memories that might explain the curse. And your part in it."

I stepped back, almost tripping over the soft dirt that still covered his grave, catching the smell of the flowers I'd placed there. He knew about that picture. "Tell me what you know now, Jackson," I said, hands on my hips. "Why do I look like that doll and who's Eliza?"

He pointed to the graves of his family. "My parents were relatively old when they had me. You may not have known that. They weren't going to have children at all because my father was convinced his children would be lost to the curse. My mother was 40 when she finally decided it was now or never and she chose now. She gave my father an ultimatum."

I nodded. It was a similar story to how I got adopted. Around 40, my mother had a "now or never" moment, and she chose adoption.

He went on. "When I met you, I was drawn instantly to you. You looked just like the doll in the closet, just like the woman who put the curse on my family so long ago. I knew there was a connection, and I felt it."

I looked up at the sky, concentrating on the clouds. "So you married me because I looked like the curse-woman?"

"No," he said, hovering by my face now. "I loved you more than you'll ever know. But your notebook full of baby names, and your mother's nagging... I knew you wanted children. I knew your 'now or never' time was coming. I couldn't give a child up to the curse. So, I chose to let you go."

"So you're trying to tell me," I said slowly, my face growing warm into anger. "That you went to strip clubs and ran around with Destiny because you were *choosing* to let me go? You're delusional. I left because you were a disgusting jerk."

I looked down at my heels, partially covered in the dirt from his grave. The very grave I should be dancing on. I could not believe he was trying to hand me the "I had to date that stripper for your own good" crap.

"I know you'll never truly forgive me for all the awful things that happened, but I think if we work together, we can help a lot of people rest in peace: ones trapped in a curse, ones trapped by their own unsolved murders, maybe even end the curse at Gate House."

He stared into my eyes, in that same ridiculous way he used to try to be cute back when we were married. I searched his face for the dimple in his cheek he used to shave around, but I didn't see it in his ghostly shadow, so I turned away and looked at my watch. It was getting late and I still had a sink full of dishes to clean and an ageless dog to feed before too long.

I wasn't sure what was happening here, not with him, the house, the curse, or the ghosts that wanted my help.

But I knew it was all going to happen over my dead husband's body.

The End

READ onto the next chapter for a sneak peek at the next book in the series called *After the Suffragette's Suicide*.

From the back of the book:

CLIENTS COME TO HER FOR ONE REASON:

**THEIR MYSTERY CASES HAVE GONE COLD,
AND SO HAVE THEY**

The second in the fun, new paranormal series The Ghosts of Landover Mysteries.

Carly was thrilled to inherit her awful ex-husband's Victorian after he died. Of course, that was before she knew she'd also be inheriting his annoying ghost, a 100-year-old curse, and the kind of strong mediumship that has every spirit in town begging for her to solve their mysteries. And Bessilyn Margaret Hind is first in line.

In 1906, suffragist and local women's rights leader, Bessilyn Hind, committed suicide at her thirty-fifth birthday party after her fiancé broke up with her. Only one problem: her ghost doesn't remember it that way. And, Bessie is appalled that books have been written about her that imply a man caused her to do something so drastic. **She didn't take her own life, and she wants Carly to find out who her real killer is (and run retractions on history, pronto).**

Through channeling, Carly is brought straight to 1906 to relive the party moment by moment, take down clues, and figure it all out. A mystery Carly gets so caught up in, she risks losing her own place in the timeline, and herself.

The Ghosts of Landover Mystery series has haunted houses, seances, channelings, curses, shapeshifters, killer birds, and a ton of mysteries. It also has mild profanity and adult humor.

Books in the series so far:
Over My Dead Husband's Body
After the Suffragette's Suicide
Behind the Boater's Cover-Up
Under the Cheater's Table (Coming Soon)
With a Ghost of a Christmas Present (Christmas novelette, coming soon)

AFTER THE SUFFRAGETTE'S SUICIDE

CHAPTER ONE: DEAD CLIENTS CAN BE SO DEMANDING

*W*orking with dead people has taught me that death is a part of life. Living with dead people has made me seriously wish there was a way to kill dead people.

That's what went through my head as I snooped around the library that afternoon, something I was absolutely certain went against the strict 75-page agreement I had to sign when I inherited this Victorian two months ago. But so far, my only regret was my shoe choice.

Those damn designer, light brown, ankle booties. I had to have them when I saw them sitting on the clearance rack, lonely and forgotten. Of course, they weren't in my section. Nothing good was ever in my section. Why did the whole world have to have a size 8?

"They're way too small," Shelby said, when she saw me twisting my foot at a strange angle to get them on. "You look like you're in pain."

"They just need to be broken in, is all," I said, because they were only ten dollars.

And now, I was breaking them in while trying not to break my neck. The library's rolling ladder swayed a little as I tried to stand on it while simultaneously running a hand along the dusty top shelf. My toes were numb and my foot slid forward every time I shifted my weight, because apparently, traction isn't included for ten dollars. But I was determined to snoop. And I figured the top shelf had to be where all the dirtiest secrets were.

I tugged another antique book from its spot, and looked it over. *Little Women.*

"Really?" I said to no one. "You hid Little Women, from who... women?"

I shook its pages with my free hand to see if anything good was hidden there, my feet slipping out from under me as I did. I grabbed the ladder just in time.

"Oh for goodness sakes, you're going to kill yourself snooping around like that," my ex-husband said, suddenly appearing in the desk chair below me. His coloring seemed strong in the afternoon light streaming in through the stained-glass windows. I could make out the dimple just above his beard. He looked up. "You could've at least worn a skirt. Made things interesting for a lonely ghost."

"Just as disgusting as ever," I said, realizing I hadn't even jumped when his ghost appeared. I was getting used to him popping in, which was a good thing; I could easily have fallen in these shoes, again. "And just so you know, dirty old men aren't considered adorable relics anymore. They're considered sexual harassers."

"But... adorable sexual harassers."

"If adorable includes getting fired, having your career ruined, or, if they're a ghost, watching as their ex-wife sparks up the sage." I put the book back on the shelf and carefully climbed down, one step at a time, staring at my slippery, cute feet the whole way.

I jumped from the last step and my landing shook the entire unstable turret, reminding me that this house was designed by a crazy man back before permits and safety were a priority.

"What are you looking for, anyway?" Jackson asked.

"Secrets."

"You'll have to be a lot more specific than that around here."

I sat down on the bright red sofa at the far end of the library and tugged off my boots, watching as my feet expanded to their natural form, like clowns from a tiny car. I opened the scrapbook in front of me on the coffee table. It was the one I'd found two months ago in this very room after the house helped me escape death.

And that scrapbook had set me on a quest to find out everything I could about the Victorian I'd inherited from my dead ex-husband, and the curse I'd apparently inherited along with it.

It probably wasn't a coincidence that I looked exactly like Eliza, the woman who had allegedly cursed the house in the early 1900s. From our curly light hair to the shape of the mole on our neck, we were the same. We even looked the same naked. I only knew that last part because the scrapbook in front of me had a photo on the last page of Eliza dancing nude on Henry Bowman's desk way back when.

But so far, that was about all I'd found out about the curse, other than the fact that I probably had a ghost for a house-keeper and a dog that seemed to be aging like Benjamin Buttons.

I closed the book before he could ask to have a look at that last page or something, and ran my finger along the gold-embossed title: *There Was a Crooked Man*. Henry Bowman had been a crooked man, all right, making his millions off of shady brothels.

"I was actually hoping to find more books like this one," I said.

Jackson glanced at the cover, his arms crossed to reveal the pretentious, ridiculous elbow patches on his jacket. "So, you want my help in your snooping?"

"I'm not snooping. I'm exploring my own house. Now, did you show up to annoy me? Because I don't have time." I looked at my cell phone to emphasize this, realizing I really didn't have time. *Shoot*. I had to be at the Purple Pony in an hour.

Jackson was just as snotty as usual. "Not that I need a reason to haunt my own house, but I actually have a bit of an announcement to make."

"You're ready to move on to a better place. I've heard that happens with dead people. See you later," I said.

"I could never do that to you, darling," he replied. "You'd be so lonely without me. Actually, I made a decision about our first client."

"Finally."

He'd been interviewing entities for the last two months, trying to decide who was worthy to be the first. I was getting a little tired of hearing about it.

He went on. "It's an honor to work with her, really. One of the oldest ghosts in Potter Grove has requested our services. Bessie Hind. She remembers my great grandfather, dear thing. Lots of stories to tell us about him, I'm sure."

I sat on the edge of my seat. Just the mention of Henry

Bowman had me interested. "What on earth does she want with a channeling, though?"

Our services had come to mean a channeling, which is an odd kind of experience where an apparition enters your body and connects with your living energy. They can take you to any day in his or her memory, and you experience it exactly the way they did — the sights, sounds, tastes, feelings. Three months ago, when I did my first channeling with Jackson, I was able to use the clues I observed to help solve the murder of some local women. I also got to eat an incredible steak.

"This ghost has been dead for a while," I said. "She can't have any connections to the living anymore. What does she want with a channeling?"

Jackson flew behind me, a wash of cold shot up my spine as he rushed toward the short stack of books partially hidden by the sofa I was sitting on.

So that's where all the good books were.

After pulling off a large leather black one with gilded writing on its spine, just like the one on the table, he returned to the sofa.

"You've been holding out on me," I said, pointing to the scrapbook.

He licked his finger to scan over the pages, even though there could not have been any spit to help the process.

"Do you know where any other scrapbooks are," I asked.

"No, sorry. Just the one." The pages blew through his fingertips. "I do know my great grandfather kept many scrapbooks, though. This is the one dedicated to his social gatherings, I think. Who knows? The old man was eccentric."

Jackson's almost-transparent finger stopped on an old society newspaper clipping. At the top was a black and white photo of a beautiful, young, light-haired woman with pale skin and doe eyes, staring off in the distance. She wasn't smiling, but no one ever did in early photographs. The date said the article came from 1906. The caption: Socialite Bessilyn Margaret Hind commits suicide.

"You would think she'd remember committing suicide," Jackson said. "I'm sure that has to be memorable."

I ignored my ex-husband's attempt at a joke and read out loud:

During her thirty-fifth birthday celebration at the home of her parents, Miss Hind suggested to her many guests that she would be taking a long trip and that this would be farewell for a while. Following cake and champagne, the socialite retired to her room alone where she was later found shot in the chest.

Due to the fact that she was found alone, and her room door and window had been locked, police determined the death to be a suicide. Friends and family say she was despondent over a recent break-up with Sir Walter Timbre of Landover and had confided that she was worried her chances at matrimony had passed her by.

Miss Hind was a champion for women's rights in Wisconsin, most notably the controversial suffrage movement, and is survived by both her parents, Greta and James Hind and her sister, Mrs. Pleasant Brillows.

"Poppycock!" a loud voice in front of us said.

I looked up, not the least bit surprised to see the same woman from the photo in the newspaper. She was a little older than she'd looked in the article, but then, the dead rarely got to choose what picture was put in their obituary. She was dressed in a silky champagne-colored dress, probably her party dress that evening, and her hair was in a loose up-do. Beautifully Edwardian looking. She was more colorful than

Jackson. I could almost see the pink in her cheeks and the blonde highlights shimmering in the overhead light.

"Bessilyn, I presume," I said.

"I want retractions," she demanded before I had a chance to even ask what she was hoping to get from our channeling. "That obituary is rubbish and I want a full retraction, pronto."

"I'm not sure they do full retractions on obituaries, but even if they did, probably not on ones more than, say, a hundred years old."

She studied my face while she floated this way and that, inspecting it. I couldn't get over how much more lifelike she was than Jackson, and he was pretty colorful today. She touched my cheek and I actually felt her cold hand vibrating over it. "You look familiar," she finally said when she'd finished studying every crack in my makeup. "When I first saw you at the Purple Pony, I noticed it. And now that I'm getting an up close and personal look, I'm sure."

I nodded, slowly. "Well, I have become quite popular among the ghosts in town, or so I've been told." I shot my ex-husband a look.

"Sorry, Carly doll. I should've mentioned she was here," he said. "She came from the bed and breakfast."

Bessie sat down on the desk chair. I'd never seen a straighter back or a more proper leg cross. "The Landover Bed and Breakfast used to be the Hind Estate, my family's home. The new owner is horrible. Paula Henkel. Dreadful, dreadful person who drives like she's asleep and snores like she's attempting to wake the dead."

"I heard the bed and breakfast is haunted. Now, I guess, I know whose work it is."

She patted her puffy hairline. "Thank you. I'll admit I had to increase my theatrics in order to get Miss Henkel to request a seance with your boss." She looked up at the ceiling. "The antics perfectly respectable ghosts must go through to impress the skeptics, really."

"So you'd like retractions," Jackson interrupted, rolling his eyes. "What is it you can offer?"

"I can tell you think retractions are foolish," she said. "But I was a women's rights leader. And believe it or not, I was quite aware I was making history at the time I was making it. I cannot have people thinking this was the message. I would never have committed suicide, especially not over a man. It simply did not happen. Therefore, I want you to figure out who my murderer was, and, yes, I want full retractions on every piece of literature that talks about my suicide." She rubbed her gloved hands together. "Shall we get started?"

Jackson held his hand up. "Hold on a second, Bessie. We talked about this. Carly needs to agree to the channeling. They're very hard on the living. Tell us what we'll get in return."

"Of course," she said. She hovered closer to me, studying my face again, turning her head this way and that. I could feel her heavy energy, and I gulped thinking about a channeling with such a strong ghost, especially one I didn't know. My boss at the hippie shop warned me not to do them at all, that they were harder on my body than I realized.

She finally spoke. "I was going to offer you a glimpse of Henry Bowman from 1906. He was at my party that night. But I think I can do better." Bessilyn was so close to my face I was surprised I didn't smell her perfume. "Because now I remember where I know you from," she said. "You're Henry Bowman's nanny. Or, you look just like her. Eliza, I believe. She was at my party, too, following the Bowmans around as usual, only there weren't any children with the Bowmans that evening. Hardly a need for a nanny, wouldn't you say?"

"Done," I said. "We'll do the channeling tomorrow."

* THANK you for checking out *After the Suffragette's Suicide,* available on Amazon.

Made in the USA
Coppell, TX
31 December 2019